MW00526286

WHEN YOUR VOICE TASTES LIKE HOME

When Your Voice Tastes Like Home

☙ IMMIGRANT WOMEN WRITE ❧

edited by Prabhjot Parmar and Nila Somaia-Carten

Second
Story
Press

NATIONAL LIBRARY OF CANADA CATALOGUING IN PUBLICATION

When your voice tastes like home : immigrant women write / Prabhjot Parmar
and Nila Somaia-Carten, editors.

ISBN 1-896764-71-1

1. Canadian literature (English)--Women authors. 2. Immigrants' writings,
Canadian (English) 3. Canadian literature (English)--21st century. I. Parmar,
Prabhjot II. Somaia-Carten, Nila

PS8235.W7W36 2003   C810.8'09287   C2003-900553-4
                          PR9194.5.W6W36 2003
                          Printed in Canada

Collection copyright © 2003 by Prabhjot Parmar and
Nila Somaia-Carten
Individual stories and poems copyright © by the authors named

Edited by Judy MacDonald
Cover by Sue Todd
Design by L. McCurdy and P. Rutter

"Arman" is reprinted with permission from *Two Sisters*, by Mehri Yalfani
(TSAR Publications, Toronto, 2000).

Christl Verduyn's poems appear by permission of the author and Guernica
Editions, taken from *Silt* (Guerica Editions, 2002).

"My-Lady-In-The-Cage" by Laurie Anne Whitt was first published in
Porcupine Literary Arts Magazine.

*Second Story Press gratefully acknowledges the support of the Ontario Arts Council and the
Canada Council for the Arts for our publishing program. We acknowledge the financial
support of the Government of Canada through the Book Publishing Industry Development
Program, and the Government of Ontario through the Ontario Media Development
Corporation's Ontario Book Initiative.*

Published by
SECOND STORY PRESS
720 Bathurst Street, Suite 301
Toronto, Ontario, Canada
M5S 2R4

www.secondstorypress.on.ca

In loving memory of Eliza Cecilia Somaia
August 29, 1934 — September 11, 1999
We miss you mum

— N. S.

For Kusum Didi and other immigrant women
a salute to their endurance and their assertion

— P. P.

Table of Contents

❈ ❈ ❈

Acknowledgments

We would like to thank Nadia Sapiro for letting us use the title of her story "When Your Voice Tastes Like Home" as the title of this anthology.

Thank you to all the women who contributed to this book for their patience and understanding. We also appreciate the keen interest and words of encouragement from women who responded to our initial call for contributions.

A special thanks to Joanne Gillespie for her encouragement. Thank you to Second Story Press for their editorial efforts and words of support. And most of all, our sincere thanks to all the contributors for their patience, support and encouragement.

Introductions

THE IDEA FOR THIS PROJECT took quite some time to develop. It began shortly after Prabhjot and I met in 1993, working for an agency that provides services for recent immigrants to Canada. Prabhjot worked with South Asian women in the Stopping the Violence program and I assisted members of various ethnic communities in my role as a family counselor. Both of us had recently migrated to Canada, and the support we provided to one another in our individual struggles to adjust to and settle in an unfamiliar country was immensely meaningful.

Aware of how we had been affected by our own experiences, Prabhjot and I became curious about those of other immigrant women. How similar were their stories? How might they differ? Did a person's age or gender influence the experience? What about ethnicity and language? The idea of inviting women to submit their immigration stories as contributions to an anthology gradually emerged as a way of gaining insight into these questions and, ultimately, of sharing this insight with others.

Some of the women in this collection recently immigrated; others arrived over twenty years ago. Some came for economic advantage; others as refugees. Yet all have written of their experiences with a clarity that illustrates their intense, detailed memories of radically life-changing events. In reviewing and selecting the contributions, we strove to balance shared experiences with those unique to individual situations. It became important, however, to acknowledge common themes. We were not surprised to identify themes of racism, sexism, ambivalence, loss and grief, challenged or lost identity, emotional and physical security and, of course, plenty of hopes and dreams both fulfilled and disappointed. Yet, while the stories share common threads, each is made unique by the individual writer's history, character and means of coping with her particular migratory experience.

Migrants and refugees who anticipate being welcomed to countries with open arms are often disappointed. Their cultural differences, especially in language, dress and custom, can be perceived as challenges to the status quo and to the comfort of longer-term residents, who can experience differences as threatening intrusions rather than as opportunities to broaden their horizons. This all-too-common interpretation of differences as threats to the status quo can contribute to the creation of an adversarial "us and them" dynamic. The arrival in British Columbia of four boats carrying 590 "illegal" Chinese migrants between July and September of 1999 is one such situation. We cannot help but wonder if the same generally outraged reaction would have been voiced if the occupants of those boats were white skinned, from an English-speaking or European country.

Racism — coupled with the notion that immigrants are a drain on society and contribute to unemployment by taking jobs from others or by living on the "system" — feeds this type of reaction. In reality, immigrants who are admitted to North America are, for the most part, not only employable and contributing members of society, but consumers as well.

People migrate, either by necessity or choice, for reasons as varied and unique as the individuals themselves. The important distinction between refugees and migrants — the element and degree of choice regarding such a critical life decision, and the presence or absence of traumatic historical experiences such as persecution or torture — has an impact on how they adapt and cope with the inevitable confusion. The term "culture shock" describes the anxiety and bewilderment experienced by those who move,

2

voluntarily or otherwise, to a cultural environment different from their origins. Culture shock involves the loss of social and professional status, of family, friends and of a familiar environment. These losses, when unacknowledged by the receiving community, whether through lack of interest, racism or ignorance, further demeans and complicates migrants' or refugees' experience.

Often, familiar ways of living are not considered acceptable in the new society. The world of some immigrants is turned upside-down. Social pressure to accept and live according to unfamiliar values and norms can lead to intense inner, or even interpersonal, conflict. It is not uncommon for otherwise peaceful families to erupt in intense and unexpected conflict soon after migrating, as the individual members find their various means of adapting to these demands. Many of the following stories give voice to the struggles involved in attempting to hold onto valued cultural traditions while striving to belong in a new and foreign culture.

Though not always uplifting reading, the pieces compiled here can provide a profound insight into the impact of migration on those who undertake it. Migrants, who feel isolated, displaced or unique in the complexity of their emotions, may find some measure of comfort in the revelation that their journeys share common themes with those of the writers they discover here.

It is our sincere wish that exposure to these stories will inspire in readers a greater understanding, admiration, empathy and respect for the cultural differences they encounter, as well as a genuine curiosity about their origins and the meaning they have for the contributors who represent those cultures.

— *Nila Somaia-Carten*

≋ ≋ ≋

※ ※ ※

A FEW YEARS AGO, during several friendly and supportive conversations, Nila and I ended up discussing our experiences as immigrant women in Canada, fairly recent at that time. Somewhere the idea came up of compiling an anthology as a way for the voices of other immigrant women to be heard. Although a number of anthologies of women's writings are available, it is difficult to find one that has an exclusive focus on the process and consequences of immigration, and that provides insight into the experiences of immigrant women. *When Your Voice Tastes Like Home* is our effort to provide such a collection.

Unlike region- or country-specific anthologies, *When Your Voice Tastes Like Home* comprises the writings of women with origins in different parts of the world. They have come from countries as far apart as Paraguay and Bangladesh, South Africa and Holland. The stories of the women represented here are very personal, but at the same time find a common ground through concerns we all share. The contributors comprise a broad spectrum of women, diverse in their experiences, origins, culture, language and age; some have published before and others took to writing for the first time in order to narrate their experiences. The issues brought out are as diverse as the contributors themselves.

We have not arranged the stories and poetry in sections, but we have tried to create a juxtaposition of themes. In many of the pieces, multi-axial issues of identity, language, struggle for survival and nostalgia emerge that underscore the complexities associated with the immigrant experience. These contributors have different linguistic as well as geographical backgrounds, and their first language is often not English. Yet, except for one set of poems translated into English for this collection, all pieces are original works in English. In some instances, the local shades their English has acquired hint at the colonial linguistic legacy shaped by native use.

4

The date of arrival in the new country is significant: it becomes a title, a day of gauging the physical setting and looking beyond it, and a particular date for leaving a past life to begin a new one. Some people immigrate using the arduous process of applying under a stipulated category: as an independent, a spouse, under family class or as an entrepreneur. On the other hand, driven by persecution, ethnic conflicts and hostile wars, many literally flee their homelands to save their lives. The initial ambivalence and the process of settlement sometimes leads to questioning of the act of immigration itself; leaving the familiar milieu one grew up in behind, whether comfortable or full of social, economic or political strife, and looking forward to a prosperous and peaceful future.

When discussing the title of this anthology, Nila and I talked several times about the primary factor that prompted us to embark on this venture: the inevitable question, Where are You From? Even after nine years of permanent residence in Canada, I continue to be asked this, deliberately or inadvertently. At first I politely answered the question, but after responding innumerable times, I spent hours reflecting on what was really behind this seemingly innocuous curiosity. Is it associated with regarding someone as an outsider, the Other, the one with a distinct accent; with geographic or anthropological inquisitiveness; or with issues of color? I suppose all options are true at one time or the other, but when I feel I am questioned because of color or accent, deep down it causes pain. A woman of color is always assumed to be "an immigrant," though I know many whose mothers or grandmothers were born in Canada. In meetings, workshops or social occasions, these women will still be asked, Where Are You From? The truth is, whether they arrived recently or long ago, most people in North America are immigrants. It's just easier for people with lighter skin or a less obvious accent to "blend in."

One of the major points of concern for an immigrant is employment. The thoughts and concerns about potential job opportunities and the type of work available begin along with the initial plans to leave home. In fact, for many, employment is the chief push or pull factor. Each year thousands dream of going to a "land of plenty," where hard work appears to result in success. And those who arrive in Canada or the United States, whatever their reasons for coming, soon fall in step with others looking for work, not only for subsistence, but also to achieve the alluring dream of a better life. Yet for a majority the employment situation after immigration is very difficult; foreign credentials are not often recognized. Doctors, nurses, architects, engineers, hair stylists and chefs find themselves having to take courses in order to attain equivalency and suitability for a particular job in their area of expertise. Many turn to any available work in order to sustain themselves and their families. Immigrant women, in particular, are often forced to accept below-minimum-wage jobs under exploitative employers. Those who find work in line with their interest or experience are few and far between.

Though immigrants contribute tremendously to the economy and society, there is a prevalent myth that they take jobs away from the "mainstream" community. In spite of the studies and reports that the government, non-profit agencies and social and political scientists churn out, nothing appears to shatter this myth. Immigrants continue to be the targets of wrath and discontent. It is convenient to falsely blame minorities for straining the economy and "stealing" jobs. When we look at job placement in Canada and the United States, of course, immigrants do occupy positions in technology, business, academic and political organizations. But the majority work in poor conditions at underpaid jobs, on farms and in greenhouses and manufacturing sweatshops, for example. Immigrant workers are most visible as janitors, taxi drivers, porters, dishwashers, etc. Do the people who complain of them stealing jobs truly wish to change places?

The emotional consequences of immigration linger

long after the actual move. The physical relocation is accomplished in the process of migration, but the mind thrives on what was left behind; by looking back, it acquires strength to adjust to its new socio-political context. In the subconscious, memories constantly play and are a strong bond with the past. Recollections and nostalgia therefore permeate through many of the stories and poems in this collection. Whatever practicalities occupy the mind during the act of immigrating, whatever outward experiences immigrant women face during day-to-day life in their new country, inevitably — invited or uninvited — thoughts of places and people left behind suffuse the inner self. We hope that *When Your Voice Tastes Like Home* gives a voice to these contributors' inner selves.

—*Prabhjot Parmar*

⚔ ⚔ ⚔

The Landing

Cristina Moretti

Landing in Canada an immigrant

September 4, 1997

is like a flat square

slippery gray building

you stumble upon,

not even

the rippled decorations of windows

to hold on to

cold glass to look inside:

some papers and light bulbs

rather than evenings

Still the ocean looks beautiful behind you

a quiet cup of silver

filled to the brim with familiar places

and vessels

from where we called ourselves homesick

only travelers

through vast lands of desires

❧ ❧ ❧

The Departure — The Arrival

Lubna Warawra

ON THAT NIGHT MY FRIEND Iman and her three children came to say goodbye to me, my father played with the children and Iman and my mother talked about things. Three-year-old Raghad was not playing, even though her older brother and sister were having a great time, being tickled by my father and climbing on his shoulders.

Raghad looked at me and said (angrily), "Auntie, don't you love us?"

I said, "Sure, sweetie, I love you very, very much."

She said, "So how come you're leaving us? What is in Canada?"

I said, "There is a better job and education for me, sweetie."

She said, "Why can't you get that here?"

I said, "Because it's different there."

I told her some stuff about the future that she didn't understand, and neither did I.

I noticed that my mother disappeared. When she came back, she had red eyes. She'd been doing that every fifteen minutes. I held myself together perfectly. That night I didn't sleep at all, I'm sure my father and my mother didn't either.

Next day we were at the airport. I can't remember how, but I found myself at the airport with my father and mother and uncle, his wife and one of my cousins. All I remember was the very heavy coat that I was wearing: I called it "the sheep." I was wearing my sheep and feeling that I was about to die from heat. I couldn't fit my sheep in either of my huge suitcases, they were full. I filled them up with things I couldn't leave behind.

It was a very long trip, to the unknown. I couldn't sleep at all. All I remember was the longest sunset in my life — it

11

was almost three hours long. This made me feel happy and optimistic. I remembered a conversation I once had with my mother: which was more beautiful, sunrise or sunset? My mother preferred sunrise because it represents a start. Well, sunset is a start too, a start of a new night and a preparation for another sunrise. I was thinking that both are beautiful, they just have a different taste of beauty and one can't exist without the other.

I arrived at Toronto's airport. My plane to Ottawa was late, so I had to stay awake. I was exhausted; I'd been up for more than thirty hours. I found sixteen cents on one of the chairs; I thought this was a sign of good luck. The immigration people gave me some welcoming brochures at the airport, and a paper that many people in the Arab world would die or kill for — my permanent residency paper.

Mary, my relative's friend, was supposed to wait for me in Ottawa. My plane arrived at 2 a.m. — several hours late. I'd never seen Mary, only spoken with her on the phone; all I knew was that she was supposed to wear a green coat. I had my sheep on, and was dragging two huge suitcases while holding my oud in my hand. There was no one waiting for me. People who were there for other people took them and left. I didn't see any green coats, or any green things at all. The only green things were my suitcases.

I stood there, not knowing what to do. Suddenly a guy came up to me and asked, "Are you Arab?"

I said — surprised — "Yes, how did you know?" (I was still naive, I didn't realize it was written all over my face, in my color, features, eyes, everything.)

The guy said, "It's obvious, you look like an Arab and you have a oud."

He asked me where I was from. I told him I was from the West Bank. He told me that he worked at the airport, and that he too was from the West Bank, from Bethlehem! I got excited and told him that I was also from Bethlehem. He asked me which high school I went to. We discovered that his wife was in my class.

12

"Isn't there anyone waiting for you?" he asked. I told him about the woman with the green coat who hadn't come.

He decided that we should call her and take directions. He was going to drive me.

On the phone I asked, "Did I wake you up?"

She said, "Yes."

I said, "Sorry."

She explained (not apologized) that the plane was late. It was past her bedtime, and she had to go to bed because she had work in the morning. I lied: "Oh, it's okay, I understand."

She asked me to take a cab, so I told her that there was someone ready to drive me.

I thought she'd say, "Careful," or something like that, but she welcomed the idea. She gave him directions. He drove me to her place.

I never saw him again in my life.

※ ※ ※

A oud is a six string instrument much like a large lute, and is played in northern Africa and southwest Asia.

13

Departure

Hoa Tran

Viet Nam Tet celebration 1975

Along with the festivities
came the blood
    that crawled out of open wounds
    taking along with it someone's soul
The war crept
    closer and closer to our home

My family and I
    were forced to leave

As we approached the huge ship
    panic suddenly overwhelmed me
All I could see was the figure of my father
    walking away

"Wait for me, Daddy!"
I could hear myself screaming
    but my lips never moved

"Wait for me!"

Desperate people everywhere
running in different directions
Chaos and madness
    suffocated me
I was so frightened
A burst of flaming tears
    poured down my face
My lungs collapsed
    into heavy breaths for air

15

I blended into the chaos
and was so terrified that
my father would not see me
and I would lose him

I ran after him
He walked faster and faster
"Where are you going?
Wait for me, Daddy!"

Hopeless words
echoed through my head

I lost one of my shoes during the struggle
I had not realized
until I heard a familiar voice
calling my name
I turned toward its direction

My mother kneeled
to pick my shoe off the ground

I turned back toward my father's direction
He disappeared among the crowd
boarding the ship

My gaze was frozen
lost and emotionless
paralyzed with fear

Suddenly a ship guard
picked me up
and threw me in a netted sack
along with other children my age
Like potatoes
We were carried from the ground
dangling in mid-air

The sack landed
    and dumped us on the floor

To my surprise
I saw my family
    and instantly
    ran towards them

Several days went by
    that seemed like years

Being on the top deck
    there was no roof
    no cover
The sky's waters
    beat against our flesh
Our scarce possessions
    were shredded by the rain
My father released them
    into the vastness of the sea

I watched
My older sister
sitting in a corner
    alone
Clutching her photograph album
    with her knuckles white
    and arms wrapped tightly

Her whole life was in that book
Most of the photographs
    were destroyed

But there was no way
    she would allow
    the ocean to swallow
    it from her

I turned away
     closed my eyes
     and held my knees
     close to my chest

The wind came
     and dried my tears
I awakened
     and looked over the rail
I could see
     the cliffs and valley
of my birthplace
     slowly fading

An empty horizon appeared
My home had sunk into the ocean

🌊 🌊 🌊

February 1, 1992

Nila Somaia-Carten

I

I LOOK OUT THE PLANE WINDOW as we circle the city before landing. It is already dark and the twinkling lights below seem to stretch out forever. I have heard Vancouver is a beautiful city and I later find out that it is, indeed, quite pretty.

The palms of my hands are sweaty and as I anxiously wipe them on my jeans, I become conscious of the many questions that are running around in my head. Will I find a job? Will I find a place to live? Will I make good friends? How will I find my way around? From up here, the city looks huge. My thoughts run on as I continue looking out the window. I question whether I am making the right decision. I worry that I am making the biggest mistake of my life.

I am going to be met by family friends at the airport. They are friends of my parents I do not really remember; family friends whom I have not seen for more than fifteen years. I will be staying with them until I settle on my own. More questions invade my already teeming head. Will we get along? What if they don't like me? What if I don't like them? How long will they allow me to stay?

I pray a silent familiar prayer, God help me, please let me be okay.

I am interrupted by the pilot asking the cabin crew to prepare for landing. I open my purse to check for the millionth time that I have all my papers. I take out the sealed envelope that is supposed to be opened only by the immigration officer. There are faint indentations on the edges. Indentations from my thumb prints, from my fingers, from the amount of time I have spent holding and staring at it. I don't believe words will ever sufficiently express what these papers represent. A flight attendant walks by and reminds me to raise my seat to the upright position.

We land quite smoothly considering the weather.

"Welcome to Canada," says one of the flight attendants as we taxi down the runway towards the gate.

I have difficulty believing I am finally here. I look out the window. Rain is streaming down the glass. All I see are fuzzy lights in the distance.

It is a relief to be off the plane. My body feels stiff and I appreciate the opportunity to stretch my legs as I walk down the corridor towards immigration. The line moves quite quickly. The immigration officer's name is Randy. I notice how dry his hands are as he tears open the sealed envelope. Mine are still damp and I hide them under the counter, hoping he won't notice them. He smiles at me as he finishes processing the papers. "Welcome to Canada," he says.

I smile back and thank him as I put the papers away, still hoping he won't notice my hands.

I am directed to customs. My heart sinks when I find out I have been misinformed by the Canadian Consulate in Nairobi regarding the goods I am bringing into the country. I find myself wanting to scream as I hear one of the customs officers telling me I have to price each and every item on my list. My three-page list of goods looks short compared to everyone else's, but I, of course, have to wait for the others in line before me. I am given a number and sit down. I try starting up a conversation with a couple, who I noticed were on the plane with me from London. They are not very friendly so after a few minutes, I give up. Maybe they, too, have worried thoughts running through their heads. I notice the woman is looking at me with some distaste. I wonder briefly if they are racist. I hope not, but I've seen that look before. It saddens me.

I start to think of my family, what they may be doing at this moment. I miss them terribly. I wish I were with them

— what I would give right now to be with them. I feel the tears welling up. *Not now, not now!* I refuse to cry in front of everyone and especially this couple sitting across from me. I stop the tears from spilling over and shift into automatic pilot. *Don't think, don't feel.* You'll make it.

II

IT HAS BEEN OVER AN HOUR and I worry that my family's friends will leave, as it is taking so long for me to get through customs. I don't even want to think about getting to their place on my own. I feel so tired. The adrenaline that has kept me going is fading fast. I shift around in my seat, hoping to find a more comfortable position. Suddenly, my number is called.

"Welcome to Canada," says the customs officer as I walk into the office.

She is very friendly and helps me finish pricing my goods. A lot of what I have are gifts from my parents, and I am having difficulty guessing the cost. As I leave the office, she wishes me luck and even tells me to come back and visit sometime. I wonder if she can tell I am on the verge of tears.

I walk out into the arrivals area and, with relief, recognize my family's friends. They have waited for me. They are not hard to miss, as there are very few people walking around or waiting.

"Welcome to Canada," they say when I reach them. They also tell me I look very much like my mother.

Again, I think of my family and feel the tears threatening to spill. Again, I am successful in holding them back. I am twenty-nine, but right now feel about eight, the age I first started attending boarding school. In the car, I struggle to pay attention to the conversation. It is cold, dark and raining hard. Why does everything seem so much more overwhelming in the dark?

At the house, I am shown my room, then we sit down to dinner. I push the food around my plate. Eating is an effort. I am jet-lagged. All I want to do is put my head down and sleep. My body feels like it weighs a ton. I ask to be excused. I say I need a shower and some sleep. Everyone is understanding. They acknowledge that I have had a long and tiring journey. *Yes, it has been. It's been a long and tiring journey.* A journey that actually began many years ago, not just yesterday when I boarded the plane. Maybe one day I will tell them about it.

As I leave the table, I thank them for their hospitality and kindness.

I take a quick shower. The hot water feels good. I wrap a towel around me and wipe the steam off the bathroom mirror. I feel disconnected from the face that stares back at me. I have the urge to reach out and touch it, but I don't. It doesn't feel like my face. It is only later, two or three years down the road, that I come to the conclusion that we migrants have many faces, many selves. How many of us wake up each morning wondering which face to put on? The self we are supposed to have left behind? Or the new self we are supposed to find in our new home? Sometimes we put on faces that we think the world wants to see. We sense society's impatience with our confusion and fear.

As I finish wiping the steam off the mirror, I am not aware that it will take me a few more years before I am able to touch the face in front of me.

Back in my room, I start to cry. This time I allow the tears to fall freely down my face. At this moment, all I feel is loneliness and fear. It scares me, the physical pain I can actually feel in my heart. It will be better in the morning, I console myself. I find myself pleading to God that it will be better in the morning. I cry until I am spent. I get into bed and switch off the light. The soft pillow cradles my head and just before I fall asleep, in my tired, foggy, half-conscious mind, I hear a voice saying, "Welcome to Canada."

❧ ❧ ❧

The First Fall

Christl Verduyn

All that first fall
while animals fattened
and thickened you
shed weight hair
thin layers of skin
wafting through autumn air
frosted brown stalks
of golden rod
Queen Anne's lace.

While animals burrowed
or fled you spread
your arms embraced
the cold so by harvest
your body was blue as
the moon a network of
veins a lattice of bones.

By the time the first snow fell
you were so light you could
have gusted away over
sleeping animals and land
across oceans back to places
you knew better could have
disappeared forever instead
you stayed still and silent
that whole first winter
waiting to spring.

✄ ✄ ✄

Journey to Canada

Asha Asher

I ALWAYS WONDER about the picture-perfect entries people make. When I visit the airport, I see the hordes of passengers arriving, makeup intact, being received by excited relatives. Hugs, kisses, pick up the bags and they are gone. Every journey I have undertaken has been unique, harried, leaving me totally frazzled. I do learn from mistakes, and on subsequent trips, attempt to ward off the difficulty encountered. However, with each journey, I find that I just have new things to learn. I haven't reached the end — yet.

This particularly convoluted journey unfolded over several months. My family received immigration papers for Canada in June. A few months earlier, I had been awarded a prestigious scholarship to study at an American university. After much deliberation, we decided that my husband, Vikram, and I would enter Canada to claim residency. I would then proceed to complete my studies in the United States while Vikram would establish himself financially. Our daughters, Ruchi, age one, and Prachi, age nine, would follow later.

Unfortunately the cut-off date for my daughters' entry fell about five weeks before the end of my semester. We tried desperately to get that date extended, but got bogged down in the bureaucratic paper forest. To avoid having to reapply for immigration, which would extend the separation of the family, my in-laws agreed to bring the girls and stay with them in Canada until I finished. We were worried about getting them a Canadian visa, but that worry was unfounded. We paid and my in-laws got their passports stamped.

However, the Canadian authorities required that the girls be accompanied across the border by one parent. We could not simply meet them at the airport on arrival and complete the formalities. So we arranged that I would meet them in New York, then fly to Toronto with my daughters and in-laws. Our finances were stretched pretty thin by then. A relative arranged for me to buy a cheap "subject-to-load" ticket. The next hurdle was the US visa for the girls. The authorities refused to allow them into the country. More paperwork, and copies of the Canadian immigration papers, long hours at the US embassy in Mumbai — finally my mother-in-law was given permission to bring the girls into the States for forty-eight hours. I would fly from Los Angeles, meet them in New York and then proceed to Toronto the next day.

The previous seven months I spent at the university had been carefully orchestrated. I managed to complete the entire course-work requirement for a master's degree and had organized data collection for the thesis requirement. The only recreation I had allowed myself during the entire time was a group dance I was to participate in at a university cultural event. I had fine-tuned the day of my journey. I was to print out the questionnaire for the data collection, make copies, put them in the envelopes all ready with addresses and stamps, participate in the dance, pick up my bags packed with gifts for the kids, and a friend would drive me to the airport. Everything had been planned to perfection, with some time gaps between every event for unforeseen eventualities.

My advisor found me waiting outside her class as planned. She had looked over the copy of my questionnaire submitted the previous night. Getting her final approval, I proceeded to the computer lab to get a printout. That's when trouble started. The breakneck speed at which I had completed all the work within the last seven months came to a screeching, grinding halt. The printer refused to print. Actually it did print out the questionnaire, but strung out some of the words across the page and ate up the others. Sweating profusely, I tried every trick that I knew, without any luck. The lab assistant on duty had disappeared and the next one was not due until seven in the evening.

Still optimistic, I went through the dance routine and went right back to the computer lab, complete with the dance costume and makeup. Luckily, universities are used to all kinds of behavior from graduate students, and no one gave a second glance. The assistant diagnosed that I had picked up a computer virus, repaired the disk, and I finally got the questionnaire printed. By now, I had just enough time to grab my bags. My friend dropped me off at the airport. He offered to wait, but I hated to inconvenience him any more than I needed to. The flight was delayed for more than two hours. When they finally announced the flight, I trudged up to the gate, thinking about how I would make copies of the questionnaire in New York.

"Ma'am, the flight is overbooked!"

"Huh!"

My brain barely registered this information. I almost proceeded to explain to him that I needed to make copies of the questionnaire for my master's thesis, when I realized he had already turned to the full-fare passengers. A "subject-to-load" ticket gets bounced if other passengers need a seat. The troubles of a grad-student mother dealing with immigration officials from two countries were not his problem. Dodging between other irate heads I managed to find out that the next flight was at 6 a.m., for which the reporting time was 5 a.m. Six hours more. I decided to wait at the airport. In my country, the airports work round the clock, and an uncomfortable chair was the only difficulty I foresaw.

Over the next two hours, the airport continued to ship out the remaining flights. And then, within a few minutes, everyone disappeared. Well, not everyone. Here I was in America's most notorious megalopolis, in a huge airport, alone with three men. Within about sixty seconds, panic set in. Of course, at that time, I thought it was prudence that prompted me to call my friend back. He fired a few choice expletives. Still, he picked me up and we drove around, my eyes open for a 24-hour photocopy place. I spotted one and asked my friend to stop. He looked at me incredulously. "Stop here, at this hour? Lady, I wouldn't walk here in the middle of the day!" (Did I clarify that he was a decade younger than me?)

Next morning, I was at the counter before the staff arrived. By then, I had dark circles under my eyes, my clothes were crumpled, and I had a woe-filled story of how I was separated from my children. Luckily, I spoke with a sympathetic older lady who promised to do what she could. She finally got me on a multi-stop flight, but I had to wait until all the other passengers had boarded. Clutching my boarding card, I recited all the prayers I knew, of whatever religion I was familiar with. That included Hinduism, Christianity, Sikhism, Jainism and Islam. Someone answered my prayers. I finally staggered into my seat, pulled a blanket over my head and fell fast asleep. If any fare-paying passenger came in, they would have to lift me bodily out of the seat.

I reached New York at six in the evening. By the time I took a bus to the Port Authority, and another one to New Jersey, it was 8 p.m. I had to lug my heavy suitcases along the interminable escalators. At one point, a suitcase got stuck in the narrow aisle and remained at the bottom, while the other baggage and I continued upward. I made a quick decision, dropped my hand baggage, and started running down the up escalator. Barely thinking about the ludicrous sight I made, I was afraid I would never see the bags I had left either at the bottom or at the top. Some supreme presence above was watching me, and a panhandler held on to my bags at the upper end, amused at my antics. I was to spread more happiness along the way before we reached our destination.

Another friend came to pick me up. While waiting for him, I noticed a group of commuters running to catch a bus. Suddenly, one of the passengers cut across and gave me a big hug. It was my daughter Prachi, now ten years old. She had grown almost six inches over the time I was away. By the time I began to hug her back, this young woman pulled back saying, "Now enough, it's cold here."

Next was a reunion with my two-year-old, Ruchi, at my friend's home. Hugs and kisses, my arms aching because of dragging the heavy luggage, back and neck stiff from thirty-six hours in uncomfortable seats, heart overflowing with joy, mind fixed on copying the questionnaire, which still had to be mailed. My friend had refused to drive me around to look for a photocopy place in Jersey City. Now he was a little overwhelmed with three other adults and two kids in his serene bachelor pad. Someone had already slammed a bathroom door shut with its lock intact, putting it out of commission. This meant that everyone had to use the only other toilet available, which was in the basement. Just the noise of people walking up and down the stairs was making him nervous.

It was 3 a.m. before I could catch up on all the news. My mother-in-law had fractured her hand three weeks before this trip. Unsure of the medical care she could access in a new country, she had the plaster cast removed the day before she left. My jaw dropped. An unhealed fracture and a toddler to take care of! On the plane, she and my father-in-law, who had never before dealt with diapers, took Ruchi to the tiny toilet. I could not comprehend how they entered the cubicle together, let alone how they could pin down a hollering toddler and execute a diaper change with three available hands.

Their tickets had allowed eight suitcases and four carry-ons, plus one diaper bag for Ruchi. My mother-in-law had filled every one of them to capacity. She is a very thrifty woman — if the airline was allowing the luggage free, she was jolly well not going to buy new stuff in a new country. So she had packed up the portable potty and the pushcart with the doll that Ruchi liked. She let Prachi wear the ski shoes that Vikram had bought about ten years earlier, just in case he needed them. Of course, Vikram's shoes were about three sizes too big for her. My mother-in-law also packed a variety of dried beans and spices that she knew were not available in the foreign lands. She would have added fresh vegetables too, but she knew that they were not allowed. Now add to this my two suitcases, my handbag and my mother-in-law's handbag with all the papers. We rearranged some of the contents because my bags were not yet bursting at the seams.

We were supposed to be at the airport at 5:30 in the morning, but we overslept. At 5:20, my friend filled his car with ten suitcases and five carry-ons, plus the diaper-bag. Because the front door on the driver's side was somehow jammed, he had to climb over me in the front passenger seat. He and I started for the airport. Once we got there, we each got a cart and unloaded the baggage. He then rushed off to get the rest of our entourage. I'd left the tickets with my mother-in-law at home, so I couldn't check our luggage in. Ruchi's diapers were with me at the airport.

By the time they all arrived, the flight was boarding. I dumped the two heaviest handbags in Ruchi's stroller, slung another two on the back, gave one bag each to my father-in-law and Prachi, grabbed Ruchi and started pushing the stroller.

All the passengers were seated on the plane. All their handbags were in the overhead bins. I dropped the kids in their seats and, still pushing the stroller, started checking every bin. Searching out stray storage space, I could feel every eye on me. The captain started his announcements explaining the route and the wind speed. He added that he had received ground clearance and was ready to roll as soon as all the passengers were seated. The whole plane burst into laughter. I turned a deep red, still trying to locate space for the last bag. Finally, the steward stowed away the stroller for me.

Ruchi was soaking wet. It had been fourteen hours since her last diaper change. We could not find any diapers — we must have misplaced them when we rearranged the luggage. Although it was a short flight, Prachi became totally disoriented by airsickness as soon as we took off. She could barely hold her head straight. The long journey from India, jet lag, the time difference, little sleep and the shock of a different civilization had taken a toll on both my parents-in-law. They responded in the simplest way all happily married couples do — they started squabbling, arguing over each action to be taken.

In Pearson Airport, we passed through immigration and customs. Someone asked me whether we had a list of all the assets we brought along. I turned to my mother-in-law. Before I could ask a question, she fired a volley of questions at my father-in-law, and he replied with a more colorful barrage. I was thankful that the officials could not understand the language. The official gave up and stamped our passports, letting us through.

Our luggage was loaded onto two trolleys. Prachi took Ruchi, with some handbags, in her stroller. My parents-in-law could not be interrupted. I left them behind. Spotting my husband, I pushed my trolley across a yellow line to him, then stepped back to retrieve both the other trolley and my in-laws, who hadn't stopped yelling at each other. But a guard would not let me go back. He said it was restricted territory and I couldn't return. I said that, technically, only the luggage trolley had crossed the yellow line. It was futile.

I gave up and shouted for my in-laws to hurry out. They did. With the wrong trolley. I did not notice it until they had crossed the yellow line. I turned angrily to the guard. "Look what you have done! Now what am I going to do with this luggage? You better go and get my stuff back. If only you had let me —" He hit his palm on his head in frustration and motioned for me to go back and get our trolley. I did. And collected the rest of the family. We organized everything and everybody into two trips to our new home.

If someone had taken a photograph of our arrival in Canada, the picture would have captured a cranky two-year-old with a dripping diaper, a lanky ten-year-old who couldn't bear the smell, but preferred her to the other baggage, an older couple disoriented and arguing about something, and me, trying to count a pile of bags. And after we were all safely through, when my husband turned to me, I asked, " Is there a photocopy place nearby? I need to copy my questionnaire."

※　※　※

My name is forever burnt ...

Amal Rana

she gave me a chambeli plant
a love gift
it was
to remind me of that place
where i once lived
to quench a tiny bit of longing
that unleashes itself in my heart
now and then

now and then
i think of you
when the chambeli flowers first
begin to bloom
i think of you
when their scent explodes upon
the latticed windows of my memory
i think of you
when i run the delicate white petals
gently down my lover's sleeping curves
i think of you

mysterious undefinable land
like you
i am full of contradictions
loving you
with a red tinge of anger and
bitterness

red like the sand hills
upon which i rolled
laughing and screaming with joy
i have that picture still
i am standing with my arms spread out
attempting to embrace your
elusive beauty
that day i took home a handful of your
rich dry grains
wanting to preserve a piece of you
forever
preparing in advance for the departure
that was inevitable
you knew before i did that we would
have to part
i was born of you
i was born in you
under your luminescent skies
and blistering desert winds
but i could not stay and be free
to live in the ways that you had taught me

the day i left i swore i would return soon
to taste your arid heat
your cool fragrant nights
to visit your ancient hills in medina
and to slice deep into your salty waters in jeddah
i swore i would carry your truth
to the outside world
so that they too could see that you were
much more than
rich oil sheiks and silently veiled women
you were a land of old blood, pagan goddess

and jinn
a land that bred me to be resilient and indestructible
to dig deep into the most hostile of soils
in order to find water to feed my soul
a land upon which my name is forever burnt
deep below the ever-shifting sands

※ ※ ※

chambeli: Urdu word for jasmine

jinn: according to Muslim scripture, the jinn were created out of smokeless fire and like humans, they are subject to the laws of birth and death. They can appear in any shape, human or animal, and can easily move between different planes of existence. Worshipped as deities by pagan Arabs before the spread of Islam, jinn play a large part in the folklore of many Muslim countries.

When Your Voice Tastes Like Home

Nadia Sapiro

THE TWENTY-FIRST OF MAY, 1994. I left my entire life behind me and began again. It was the day when I said, "N'kosi Sikelele I'Afrika" — G-d Save Africa — as I left my homeland of South Africa and emigrated to Canada.

When my family arrived here we drove from the airport to our new accommodations. All I saw were square little boxes. I was not going to live in one of those; our home would be better. Later, I visited my parents' friends' homes. They looked to me like renditions out of a cubist gallery. The malls were huge, with uniform stores lining the walls, expensive merchandise and well-trained salespeople cajoling me to buy, buy, buy.

The high school that I visited was ugly, angular, old. It had a strange smell. All the people around me sounded like extras on the cast of "Beverly Hills 90210." When I began school I heard, "You have such an unusual accent," so many times. People I didn't even know would walk up to me and ask me to talk. They loved hearing me say, "Plant, Dance and Bananas in Pajamas." I sometimes felt like a parrot, yet I still talked for them and continued to smile because my voice was one last link with home.

The guidance counselors had no clue how to help me or what to tell me. They tried to organize me, but they did not understand the place I had just left.

The teachers kept saying to me, "You are so polite."

I, on the other hand, thought that everyone else was just so rude.

My brother, trying so desperately hard to fit in, started putting on a Canadian accent. I was trying to avoid acknowledging my own misery. After all, we had a democratic family vote, and I had voted to come to Canada; to be free from the political instability and violence that plagues South Africa. And now — how could I complain about my own choice?

My birthday that October was the most bittersweet one that I have ever experienced. When my childhood friends called, I cried on the phone, "I hate it, I want to leave this place so much, I want to come *home*." At two dollars per minute, hearing my best friend halfway across the world say, "It will get better," is like trying to fix internal bleeding with a Band-Aid. But I made my friends a promise that I would give myself a chance to like this place called Canada.

I now have many friends and responsibilities to fill the void created by leaving South Africa. My accent is kind of fading, now that several years have passed since I arrived. I've built a life with people who I hope would care, should I ever move again. I love Canada. I am proud to call it home. But when someone hears me talk, gives me a look and asks me, "Where are you from?" I am proud to say, "I am South African."

Tomorrow

Mehri Yalfani

On the verge of
giving birth to
    tomorrow
the world is too old.

Tomorrow
    a day
with a history unwritten
but
predictable in the media
with colors of
exciting crime
    torture
    genocide
or
some fun —
having sex with
    innocents.

Tomorrow a day
    cloudy
with a feast for trees
showering in acid rain
or
angry flood washing away
old memories of
old houses — and
a TV reporter will be
    happy
flying over tiny houses
drifting in muddy water.

Tomorrow a sunny day
with UV rays
naked bodies on azure
beaches
enjoying being tainted with
    cancer
and get rid of tomorrow —
the beautiful tomorrow.

Tomorrow I'll make a
    shade
of dead trees and
burned branches
sing a song for a
    creek
flowing – far away
from tomorrow
beautiful tomorrow.

✍ ✍ ✍

Immigration

Edith Samuel

MY HUSBAND, two children and I hail from Madras, South India. In the 1990s, my husband had a good job in a senior management position. I did not work outside the home as I had to take care of the children and my aged father-in-law. We had a comfortable life. But still I cherished the thought of migrating to the West for a better life and to give our children an excellent education.

It was a difficult decision for us to make when our papers for migration to Canada came through, though. My husband was reluctant to give up his good job and to leave his father. Since my sister-in-law was willing to look after her dad, and I was adamant that we should take the chance, we finally made the decision to leave Madras.

We made full enquiries about life in Canada and, in particular, about Toronto. We were told that jobs were available in the city, even if at first we would have to start from scratch. We felt that, if we worked hard, we could soon be financially self-sufficient. Since we had this rosy picture in our minds, we were quite unprepared to face the complications that came up.

We had no close relatives in Toronto, so we had to rely on friends for rudimentary help. They helped us with accommodations, with getting a bank account and health cards, and with settling the children in a nearby school. We needed warm clothing for the cold weather as well.

The first year was the worst of all. We lived in a basement apartment with no furniture — with meagre financial resources and unemployment looming large, we thought it wise not to buy any. My children bore the brunt of the change, but they did not complain. They somewhat liked the school and the atmosphere there. My son was thirteen and my daughter was twelve at the time — very impressionable ages, indeed.

My husband felt humiliated that he was unemployed and tried hard to find a job. Friends advised him to take any job, as the recession had just set in. We hadn't been told about any recession when we were in India. The stress of unemployment made both of us despondent and depressed most of the time. The children, even though they felt the change, did not openly show it, as they were busy in school. But my husband and I wondered whether we had made the right decision. We were prepared to go back in three months if he did not get a job. But friends advised us to keep trying.

After two months of desperate searching, my husband got a job as a sales associate in a department store. The pay was meagre, but we were somewhat relieved. I had to get a job as well. I managed to find work in a bank — but could not last at that job due to the pace of work and the surveillance there. I then landed work as a daycare teacher. Even here, the politics and job-monitoring was intense, so I decided to change once more. I went from job to job, but did not survive most of them. One of the serious problems I have faced so far has to do with the sabotaging of my work and unnecessary picking on even small mistakes. My manner of speech has often been misinterpreted and misconstrued. To this day, I am not settled in any job.

Had my master's degree, along with my ten years of teaching experience, been recognized here, I would have taken less time to settle down. I could have been accepted with ease into the teaching program and would have been a certified teacher by now. However, I was not admitted into the teaching program. Fortunately, my husband's degree was recognized and he only had to take a qualifying exam.

As a family, we were thoroughly disoriented. The loss of social status was unbearable. Since my children were used to a comfortable life in India, with all their needs taken care of, they, especially my daughter, were really affected by the change. They were not adequately provided for in matters of clothing or recreational needs, and the difference tore them apart. They were exposed to liberal Canadian values in school — my daughter, in particular, rebelled against our traditional ways of discipline and mannerisms. Both children did not want to be seen with us, and refused to go out anywhere with us. Our daughter was profoundly influenced by her peers in school and soon started to be disrespectful and disinterested in academics. She hung out with the wrong crowd, came home late from school, started smoking and wanted to date boys. These changes in my daughter's behavior led to considerable tension and strife within the family.

Many immigrant families contend with these issues, and sometimes they need professional help. In our case, we sought the help of school counselors and the pastor of our church. Still, the problems dragged on throughout my daughter's teenage years.

As a family, we had few friends and absolutely no relatives. Due to financial constraints, we were not in a position to socialize. The only friends we had were those we met in church and a few whom we spoke with on the telephone. The children did not bring any of their friends home, as they were ashamed of our changed social status and the differences in cultural values. We did not join any of the ethnic associations because of the fees attached to membership and participation in activities. As well, some of these associations are very traditional in their outlook and maintain an oppressive atmosphere in social events. The few friends who did care advised and helped us.

As Christians, we have been members of a nearby church. Even in the church family, we have not been fully accepted. Some families, who understand immigrants, are good to us, but others are indifferent. Some look down on us with suspicion, as if we cannot be trusted even in the company of children. The situation is so ridiculous at times that we do not socialize with members; we are apprehensive about saying something wrong by asking personal questions. They do not realize that we come from a traditional society and that we only wish to be friendly. Our friendliness is completely misunderstood and taken for inappropriateness.

We were completely unprepared for the racial discrimination that we have experienced so far. My brothers had warned me about racism. However, the subtleties of it emerge only as we confront various situations in day-to-day life. Indeed, it is a lived, everyday experience.

Racism begins to work from the time one applies for jobs, until one secures the job and tries to maintain the position. Discriminatory emotions affect many situations in varying degrees of intensity. Racist feelings in relationships reach such a peak that the situation ends, in most cases, very unpleasantly. In my case, I have experienced discrimination in many jobs. Even though I try to be very pleasant and do my best to learn the job quickly, some hindrance or job surveillance prevents me from settling down in an amicable manner. A supervisor or another person in charge picks on me over trivial mistakes I make, and I am soon let go in an unjust, unpleasant manner. This has been my oppressive experience from time to time. It has demoralized me, made me feel unworthy and unwanted, left me with a low level of self-esteem.

Some South Asians in higher positions do not help newcomers in any way, either. Petrified, they take sides with members of the dominant group to protect their own positions. This has been my dismal experience several times. South Asian immigrants who have lived in Canada for more than twenty or thirty years have different values and are more integrated than new migrants. Some settled immigrants show little sympathy and concern for the newcomers and, on the contrary, ridicule and belittle their mannerisms.

In academia, we have come across discrimination in the way essays are marked or in the student-professor relationship. Our children have experienced biased attitudes exhibited by some of their teachers, but they do not discuss the situation with us for fear we'll be upset.

My family is in a transitional stage, neither here nor there. We have not yet fully integrated into mainstream society. Our progress in settlement has been very slow — much slower than we had anticipated. The economic recession has had a great deal to do with our level of integration. In any case, we are taking life as it comes, and we are dependent on God to continue to guide and lead us. Our immigrant experiences have profoundly strengthened our faith in God.

※　※　※

Memsahib, Your Brown Skin

Farah Mahrukh Coomi Shroff

Memsahib
Your brown skin betrays you
Campaigning in the streets for justice
Sloganning Chanting Ranting
    Panting   S
                    l
           a
           n
              t
                  i
                  n
                  g   Sloping
Down the slippery street
As you enter your home your palace
I clean cook shop childraise nurture
for you

The Re-production of class relations
Machinations of the domestic sphere
Tribulations Stipulations Beatings

My life, Memsahib, is the horror
Of which you write and speechify
Unions are created for people who
Don't work for you
So why spew
The garbled rhetoric
Of double speak, oh so oblique!
Unidos en la lucha! Workers Unite!

Upper caste "activist feminist"
I have become your wife
My life is filled with the strife
Of your bourgeois contradictions
Convictions Capitulations Articulations

I have allowed the Indira Gandhis, Benazir
    Bhuttos
Of the world to emerge
Long before Kim and Maggie T
Splurged

South Asian bourgeoisie
My blood is on your hands

≪ ≪ ≪

Her

Aida Mashari

I myself was young
And easily did I fit in
In a strange land
With strange ideals
But her pains I felt
Her tears of anger
Her cries of frustration
I did understand.

I had not yet formed
My world was incomplete
I took in all around me
As all I ever knew
Her world
Her memories
Were bursting from her
So different from all else.

The hardest part I saw
Was changing the way her lips moved
Without forgetting
How they had moved before
Desperately trying to hold on
To parts of herself
Though they stretched
Across many miles of earth.

For she was two people
One confident
And one cautious

One melancholy
And one unable to express feeling
Both fighting for dominance
Over a single soul
That can only take so much.

It's not like riding a bicycle
Where it is at first impossible
Then suddenly
The easiest thing of all
For it never becomes that easy
But it does become easier
With patience
And time.

Just hold on tight
Push with all might
Use all the lessons
Ever learned
From anywhere and everywhere
And don't forget life's dreams
And remember to smile
For you only live once, dear mother.

⚜ ⚜ ⚜

Mrs. Akbar

Mariam Pirbhai

"I'M GOING OUT, MUM," Aliya wailed from the foyer, wrapping a long woollen scarf around her neck. "Why couldn't we live somewhere warm," she grumbled under her breath. Where she didn't have to hide behind a sea of endless layers, where she could make a quick, clean exit before her parents intercepted her getaway between bootlace tying and the ritual search for the ever-evasive glove.

"Going?" Her mother's startled voice could be heard between kitchen and foyer. "Where are you going? It's late. Your father will be home soon — and the Guptas are coming to dinner."

Mother and daughter were now facing one another by way of the foyer mirror. Since it was too late to avoid her mother's interrogation, Aliya decided she might as well take the time to touch up her lipstick and brush out her hair. Seeing Aliya standing before the mirror, her long dark hair falling heavily past her shoulders, her chocolate almond eyes lined dextrously in black, Mrs. Akbar mistook her daughter's image for of her own. Instinctively, taking the brush from Aliya's hand, she began to run it through the harder-to-reach tendrils at the back of what could just as well have been her own tangled mane.

"Please don't go, *beti*," she pleaded gently. "Your father will be cross. Besides, Mrs. Gupta looks forward to seeing you whenever she comes."

"So you want me to suffer through an entire night of Mr. Gupta's twenty questions and Mrs. Gupta's sporadic comments about *How grown up you are, Aliya!* and *How lucky your mother is to still have you to help her out at home, Aliya*. I don't think so, Mum!"

51

"Aliya, it's Christmas Eve!" replied Mrs. Akbar, changing her tack.

Aliya yanked the brush out of her mother's hand and began to brush out her hair in furious, sweeping gestures, keeping her back to her mother all the while.

"Christmas Eve! We're Muslims — or have we forgotten?" she teased, assuming the tone and head-tilting gesture of her father. "And since when did the Guptas start celebrating Christmas?"

"Since their children left, Aliya, and since Christmas is the only time Lukna and Jimmy can make it back home."

"All the more reason for the Guptas to stay home tonight with their precious Call-Me-Doctor-Jimmy and Little-Miss-Look-At-Me-Na-Lukna! Who's Javindar kidding, anyway? Does he really think that he'll get more patients by changing his name? That by being less Indian he's more doctor? They'll still have to trust a brown man with sharp instruments! Anyway, hasn't he heard about the new alternative craze? He'd do far better cashing in on his alternativity while the herbs are hot. Yeah, Mum, the more I think about it, the less I want to be here tonight. I get on Mr. Gupta's nerves, anyway."

"Aliya!" Mrs. Akbar scolded, struggling not to chuckle. Kamala Gupta did have a tendency to boast about her children's Ivy League qualifications and their fine marriages into fine families with even finer credentials. And she'd never liked this name-changing business. Tariq and Krishna had even had a big argument about it once. She remembered how she and Kamala had tried to intervene when their husbands' tempers started to veer out of control. That night, she had told Tariq that she thought the Guptas were good people, no matter what, and she wished Tariq would remember this each time he and Krishna quarreled. After all, Javindar's new name was only one of many heated topics over which they and the Guptas argued. How many of their political exchanges had led to an abrupt end to dinner? India-Pakistan relations were undoubtedly something the countries had to continue to work through, she would always say, but did they have to immigrate with history still bearing heavily down upon their own backs? Did their friendship not say something much greater about the culture they shared? How else could they explain the fact that they were each other's only friends in this new city of thousands? Anyway, Javindar's decision was his and his alone. And surely a father's first instinct would be to defend his son's choices when they were so clearly under attack, no matter what he may think about them privately.

Mrs. Akbar put her hand to her chest, as if Aliya had dredged up something that she preferred to keep at bay: "Aliya, you know very well that Lukna and Jimmy don't always make it home for Christmas. Lukna just got married —"

"*Just* got married?" Aliya howled, rolling her eyes. "Lukna's been married since she was nicknamed Lukna, for God's sake! Even her B.Com. was a glorified personals ad. She was aiming for an M.B.A., of course, but a club's a club. Before you know it, she and Mr. Lukna will be popping out their own little brood of bankers and stockbrokers through those cellular phones they seem to enjoy holding more than each other."

"Aliya, that's not the point! Mrs. Gupta misses her children, and now you're the closest thing she's got to a daughter around here."

"*Bichari*," Mrs. Akbar added, genuinely depressed for her friend. After all, the thought of her own daughter's move away from home was nothing short of emotional battery. Poor Kamala had had to accept Lukna's departure as a normal rite of passage; her daughter was getting married. And, yes, many girls managed to swindle years away from home for an education. Mrs. Akbar had no quarrel there. Hadn't she always encouraged Aliya to study dentistry? They were so independent, those dentists; they set their own hours, took long vacations, charged heaven and earth for a filling or a cleaning, and their children never had to worry about the cost of braces.

But not her Aliya! Her daughter wanted to leave home for no reason at all. Oh, of course, she wanted to be an artist! To sing! And nobody doubted her talent for a minute; certainly not her parents. Yet surely even a singing career could be more easily digested by all parties concerned when one was sure to have a well-fed tummy? Why hadn't Aliya at least inherited some of her mother's cooking savvy? They could have gone into business together by now. How many times had she tried to pry Aliya away from those disastrous headphones to coax her into the kitchen and have her try her hand at *chapatis*, or her favourite chicken *korma*? Now she'd just be another one of those Kraft Dinner kids and, one day, God forbid, Kraft Dinner mothers. Or worse, she'd be picking up all the wrong tips from that Madhur Jaffrey and her insufferable cookbooks!

But poor eating habits weren't the worst of it. In another few months, Aliya would just pick up and go to some dingy apartment, and work at all kinds of ungodly hours for what she had the irksome habit of referring to as a "gig." To think, her daughter would be working in the kind of place she couldn't even tell Kamala about. How many arguments had they all already had about Aliya leaving home? For how many months had her father assumed the silence of victory — as if his word was final and nothing more need be said — until Aliya had willed him into submission? Imagine, her own father, *willed* into submission! She was their only child, after all. Thoroughly spoiled. There were two pampered bulls in the Akbar house, but one of them had a soft spot for the other's need for independence. What about *her* independence, Mrs. Akbar thought sadly. Where was *her* say in all this?

Independence! Mrs. Akbar scoffed inwardly. Oh, Aliya's father would pretend he had reconciled himself to the idea, even go so far as to commend himself for his liberalism and magnanimity that only she, his wife, could see through. For it would be *she*, Nasreen Akbar, Mrs. Tariq Akbar, he would berate, *blame* for not having raised their daughter properly; for having been a bad example; for having never worn *hijab*. *Hijab*! In their day, who even wore *hijab*? A *dupatta* and a conscientious dose of modesty, yes; but more than this?

It was only here in this snow-covered place that their young girls were being told to cover their frost-bitten heads, one way or another. But still, at whom would he accusingly point his finger when people asked where in God's name Aliya was if she wasn't in university, if she wasn't home, if she wasn't married, if she wasn't visiting some wing of the Akbar clan in Karachi or London, if she wasn't —

"Goodnight, Mum," Aliya said, kissing her mother's cheek.

Mrs. Akbar stared blankly at her daughter for a few minutes, unable to recognize the image before her. Aliya had rolled her hair into a bun and tucked it out of the way under a black and white toque. With Aliya's hair lost under a layer of woolly fuzz, the angular jaw she had inherited from her mother seemed more pronounced than her father's rounded features. How was it that she had never before noticed the sharpness of her own face, Mrs. Akbar mused. With her hair pulled back like this, Aliya could just as well have been the son she had never had. Why had she never had a son, a brother for Aliya? Had the shock of this country frozen her marriage in time? She hadn't exactly been beyond her years when they had landed here. Maybe a brother would have been exactly what Aliya had needed all these years. Kamala always bragged about Lukna and Jimmy's great friendship, although, if truth be told, there was little show of affection in Jimmy's — Javindar's — somewhat inebriated words of well-wishing at his sister's wedding reception.

Aliya had always joked that with a brother like Javindar, Lukna could have used a few friends. But at least Lukna *had* a brother at her wedding. Family was what counted in the end. Aliya would understand this when it came time for her to marry and she needed people around her to whom she didn't need to explain her customs and her traditions. Of course, Aliya had no shortage of friends, but who among them really knew her, who among them really respected her heritage enough not to ruin her name by insisting on calling her Al? And why did Tariq have nothing to say about the fact that his own daughter's name was on the brink of extinction, much less Javindar's?

If only Aliya and Lukna had hit it off, Mrs. Akbar sighed. At least then she would have had a surrogate sister. Aliya was so different from Lukna. Lukna would never wear a hat like that, all tight and boyish. Why did Aliya have to wear that hat? It didn't suit her. Or was the mirror the problem? Personally, she never liked this mirror. It was too long; it made everything look drawn in and stretched out from bottom to top. Maybe she would buy a new mirror tomorrow. Maybe Kamala and she could go shopping. But Aliya liked the mirror. She said it made her look skinny. Aliya was thinner than she needed to be. If anything, she needed to gain a few pounds. Why were people so obsessed with being thin in a country where a few extra pounds of weight were exactly what one needed to ward off the cold? That's what they all needed here: a second skin.

"*Ummi-ji!*" Aliya tried to get her mother's attention again. "I said goodnight! Say hi to Dad and give my *salaams* — I mean, say Merry Christmas — to the Guptas for me," she continued, swinging a backpack strap over each shoulder.

Seeing Aliya heading for the door, Mrs. Akbar felt that this would be the last she would ever see of her daughter, as if she had already lost her. But lost to what, she still couldn't quite fathom. A music career? A dingy apartment she would eventually tire of? What? What?

"What?" Mrs. Akbar piped out unintentionally.

"God, Mum! I said 'I'm going' at least a million times!" Aliya yelled back over her shoulder, now halfway out the door.

Mrs. Akbar continued to feel out of sorts, her body

56

hardening like Christmas cake in a tin someone had forgotten to secure the lid on, her mind reeling forward into another new year of feeling as if someone had deliberately left her out in the open, leaving her skin to flake, her thoughts to stale.

"*Beti,*" she finally ventured, now in a faint mutter, virtually a whisper, "You never told me *where* you're going."

"Just to a friend, Mum," Aliya replied, her voice quivering ever so slightly under the veil of the lie.

"Which friend, *beti*?" Mrs. Akbar persisted.

"Mum, I thought we'd been through this before. I'm long past puberty, or hadn't you noticed!"

"It's a boy, isn't it?" Mrs. Akbar continued, uncertain as to whether she was referring to the moment at hand or to her daughter's motivation for her imminently permanent departure.

"A boy!" Aliya mimicked. "God forbid, Mum. You know I can't stand boys. Now, a *man*! That would be another story!"

"Aliya!" Mrs. Akbar reprimanded, her arched brows raised to unimaginable heights.

Aliya moaned inwardly. Had she not wanted to make a quick exit to avoid precisely this sort of ridiculous confrontation? Still, she refused to spend another night feeling guilty about this-that-or-the-other — she didn't even know what anymore: hurting her mother's feelings, abandonment, not helping with dinner, hating Mrs. Gupta for making her mother feel inadequate about everything from her own kid to her home décor ... One of them had to behave rationally, at any rate.

"I was just kidding, Mum. I won't be out all night — you know that. I'll call if anything out of the ordinary should happen — but nothing ever does and nothing will tonight — and I'll be back before Santa makes it down the chimney, I promise. Now please let me close the door before you freeze and before I miss my bus!"

Mrs. Akbar remained silent, dissatisfied and cold. Her

daughter still hadn't answered her question, any of her questions. Instead, Mrs. Akbar had been forced to humiliate herself again; forced to take another step back behind the precarious threshold of her love; forced to treat her daughter like a child when she hadn't wanted to. Of course she didn't think Aliya was a child! If anything she should have been married by now, with her own children, her own family. In case she hadn't noticed! Of course she'd noticed! Who had admired her for the way she had stood her ground, woman to man, with her father till *his* had been the losing argument?

But she was tired now; tired of a battle she had not been trained by her own mother to fight. How could her mother have prepared her for a battle to be played out on alien territory? This was a treacherous, slippery terrain; covered with so many invisible patches of ice that both mother and daughter had had to learn to walk again before ever learning how to take up arms. Only Aliya was the better learner here; her footing so much steadier than her mother's. And then it was Mrs. Akbar who was left struggling to hold on to her daughter and her every word in this shifting territory. But it was no use. Even Aliya seemed to totter about like an old woman sometimes. No, she had nothing to hold on to here. Nothing to hold on to but the poorly articulated sound of her own defeat; the kind of defeat she would later dream about in a language she had barely wrapped her own tongue around, like a poorly wrapped scarf on a biting Christmas Eve.

"Don't wake your father when you come back, whatever you do," Mrs. Akbar heard herself mumbling as she closed the door. Drifting back into the warmth of her kitchen, Mrs. Akbar stoically turned her thoughts to dinner with the Guptas and Kamala Gupta's endless prattle about her perfect, absent children.

🏮 🏮 🏮

Indian Woman I

Veena Gokhale

I dot my forehead
slip into a chudidar
dreamy against my skin
bare my belly in a sari
under my winter coat
in Toronto

South Asian Woman
presumed oppressed
(passivity optional)

At Pearson Airport
a blonde model
screams from the cover of New Woman
How about a make-over, baby?

Landing at Sahar Airport
I want to avoid the lascivious stares
of men in uniform
and men without

But force myself to hold their gaze

I am liberated ain't I?

                                                ✄ ✄ ✄

Rice Krispies Soup

Jin Lee

To my uhm-mah and ahp-pah, whose constant love and support I cannot live without. To my only oh-bah, Ernie, whose laughter has filled my life with joy.

the blue and jade colored ceramic bowl
holds my rice krispies soup
but my rice krispies do not float like Kellogg's
some swim alone, but others stick together
some even lazily rest on the bottom

my rice krispies soup tells me a story
it does not shout snap, crackle or pop but remains silent
you will find no milk in my rice krispies soup
the base is as viscous as 2% milk, but not as white
it has not been milked from a cow, but skimmed from fat
    that's patiently boiling
my rice krispies were not made from a factory in America,
    but from a pauper farm in Korea
they were not made by some noisy metallic machine,
    but by a quiet, humble woman
they were not picked by underpaid laborers,
    but by the callused hands of
a woman whose strength bore eight children, raising them
    on a farmer's income

my rice krispies are not rice krispies, you see
they are the fruits of my grandmother's work
carefully picked from finely combed rice fields in Pusan
cooked and flattened by weary hands into almost perfect
    oval shapes
served with unspoken love, traditionally on New Year's
    Day

61

so you may eat your rice krispies purchased from Loblaw's
     with pasteurized milk
crunch on them as you may please
I shall eat my rice krispies soup made by my nurturing
     grandmother
savoring her image down to the last rice krispie
in my blue and jade colored ceramic bowl

❧ ❧ ❧

*This poem describes the Korean custom of eating "duck gook," or
rice cake soup, which is traditionally served on New Year's Day.*

Chai Time

Shamila N. Chaudhary

RESTLESS, I lie awake in the gray, dusky, Midwest morning; hearing the normal, usual footsteps of Mommy in the kitchen upstairs. She is making chai for Daddy and herself. It is almost time for them to go to work.

The door opens slowly and shuts even slower. I know she will now come and sit on my bed, next to my supposed-to-be-sleeping body, and start running her fingers through my hair and pat my back. She does. "Is everything okay with you, is everything okay with you?" she repeats twice, and then a couple of more times. Then she asks if I am awake. She does not ask if I am awake before she asks me if I am alright. We are used to this routine. It is an old friend, and an old enemy.

Before, I was telling myself, you are going to be okay, you are fine. There is nothing wrong with someone who gets rid of old things. There is nothing wrong with such a person. There will be no roots for you. Dusty things collecting more dust will only make you cringe, make you sneeze. Did I not hear once or twice that when you sneeze, it means there is a jinn inside you? I must have many jinn. (Not after I get rid of all these old things!)

Mommy says she wants to friend me. She means she wants to be my friend. I always insert the verb, sometimes adjust a pronoun, and always delete the explicit adjectives reserved only for the kind of girl I am. Which, in context, are wholly negative, but somewhere might exist as extremely positive and uplifting remarks. Not for this Pakistani girl, in this Pakistani family, in this American life.

She wants to friend me. If there is something wrong with me, I should tell her. She says it seems something happened to me, something happened. It changed me, she said. I got rid of everything. I seem sad.

It seems, at first, she wants me to say I have a person in mind. To say I have someone, to admit to pre-marital interaction and interest in the male sex. I stop myself from scolding my mother. There is greater concern in her words. She keeps her hand on my tired back. She does not insist on an answer. She wishes for my peace, I know. These days are marked with laughter and understanding. My loneliness and new-found seriousness have brought my mother back to me. I want to friend her too.

Mommy already knows what I am trying to hide from her and from myself. Her sixth, seventh and eighth senses always read my face before I can. I remember to think of her as a feminist role model. Her eyes worn from twenty years of waking up early to make chai for Daddy and herself. I used to listen to their discussions and arguments in the early hours of the morning. In those days of marriage talk, and now in these days of my liberation, and their chai time and fajr prayers.

※ ※ ※

Entranced

Christl Verduyn

les extrêmes se touchent
the father says
curving over
his work
words born
died
carved in stone

chisel and hammer
he shapes words
foreign to him

for me words
a new world

fingers lingering
I trace letter
by letter

let her
learn them
as I make them
says the father
to the mother

and I enter language
as my father
engraves
it is a beginning
this engraving

I am enthralled
wholly
entranced

❈ ❈ ❈

The Awakening

Hope

SHE WAS AWAKE, wondering what woke her up. Some noise, some movement. Strange how a noiseless movement can wake you up. She saw the shadow creep up, ever so noiselessly, and reach the cradle. What cradle, when did that get here? And the shadow reached to touch the baby. She did not realize there was a baby inside the cradle, it was so silent. She tried to move towards the cradle but her limbs were strangely lifeless, and the shadow was quick, silent, but moving swiftly. The shadow had its edges curled round the baby's neck and now she could hear, no, feel, actually feel, the shadow tightening around the baby's neck. The baby did not whimper or make a sound, yet she could feel soundless screams rising and crashing.

She could not move her arms and legs; they had frozen, were encased in cement. She struggled to scream and could feel the same shadow cutting off her air, tightening around her. Why wasn't anyone helping?

Bright lights, the shock of a warm washcloth on her face.

"What's her name?"

In the background, a muffled answer.

"Time to wake up," the same brisk voice. "You are in the recovery room."

"Hurts," she managed with an effort.

"I know, the ligation is very painful, I'll give you some more sedative."

Darkness and oblivion.

And again the shadow was slowly, silently creeping up, strangling, throttling, cutting off her airway. And she heard pitiful whining. With a start, she realized it was her own voice, whining, gasping for air. Finally, the voices came close and moved her. At least she could breathe better, but her limbs refused to respond. What if the shadow returned?

What happened to the baby in the cradle?

With an effort, she opened her eyes. He was sitting on a chair near the bed. It was a different bed. He was reading a magazine, which was strange. He was not into reading, least of all a trashy magazine; the kind doctors and hospitals keep in their waiting rooms.

And she floated off again. She was younger, very plain, very simple, a freshman in college. To her surprise, one of the most popular college hunks wanted to borrow her notebook. Not just once, he wanted to refer to it regularly, he was apparently trying to improve his grades. His popularity grades were not wanting, so why was he asking for Miss Plain Jane's book? There never was a dearth of girls hanging around him. Why was he crossing her path in the most unexpected places — at the ornithology meeting? At the science committee meeting? At the library, right next to her favorite window spot. Incredible! Without his entourage too.

Before she knew it, they were taking the same bus home. And then were making wedding plans and dreaming impossible dreams. He was going to study abroad. He told her to change her major so she could work easily in a foreign land. He had a way to make the impossible happen. Two years later, they were married and on their way to Europe. Although his grades were abysmal, he had completed an innovative project in his spare time. This impressed a foreign university enough to give him a full scholarship. They borrowed money to pay for the airfare, confident they would pay it back later.

The next few years were bittersweet. The scholarship appeared to be huge when converted to their local currency. In their naiveté, they did not figure in the cost of living in the foreign land. Living hand to mouth, she looked for any kind of work available to students. Never having lifted a soiled spoon in her parental home, she now worked in a cafeteria, clearing leftover food from dishes before they were loaded into the dishwasher. She could not eat before work, afraid that the mess of leftover food would make her throw up, and she would lose the job. She spent hours babysitting, washing garbage cans in public, stuffing envelopes, any kind of job that would add to their income. And he studied and planned wild sightseeing trips.

On a shoestring budget they traveled to distant corners of Europe, staying with other students they met, camping in tents. His easy camaraderie opened doors for them. And when they returned from these adventures, she went back to work, thankful that no one they knew would see her engaged in shameful menial labor. On the evenings she was not babysitting, they dreamed of the time he would finish his studies and get a job. She could go back to school or perhaps start a family. She was content to let him plan their future.

Their first child was a complete accident. She was delighted. Through the nausea and vomiting, she looked at the pregnancy as a symbol of the deep love they shared. He looked at it as a disruption of his plans, an impediment to his career. He went into a depression, refusing to talk to her. What should have been the happiest time for them together, was for her, the loneliest. She could not bear to share the news of the event with the distant family. Perhaps they would be happy; his parents would surely welcome their first grandchild. But if the father of the child could not share the joy of creation, how could she share it with anyone else? Sometimes he accompanied her for checkups, yet she felt as though she went through all the phases of her pregnancy alone. She felt as close to him as she would to a passenger traveling on the same bus.

Six weeks before her due date, he mailed home a crude pencil drawing of her ballooning figure. The response was tremendous. Her father used up his savings to send her mother to care for her, as was the custom. His parents sent lots of gifts and traditional sweets that could be shared with friends and neighbors. And he basked in all the attention. And he adored their first born, spending every possible hour with the child. Friends envied her; fatherhood came so easily to him.

She basked in their attention and knew he was special. The earlier months were forgotten in this new-found joy.

The pain broke through the drug and brought her back to consciousness. He was still sitting there. He saw that she was awake and went back to his reading. She desperately wanted to talk to someone; perhaps a voice would make these thoughts go away. She remembered the shadow and the baby. Where was the baby and what had happened to her? Her throat still felt raw and raspy. She attempted to speak. Just then a nurse walked in.

"I see you are awake. I want you to take a drink. Keep taking small sips. As soon as you can urinate on your own, we can send you home. I'll help you sit up."

She wanted to ask the nurse what happened, but as she tried to sit up a wave of dizziness almost blacked her out.

"Easy now," the nurse steadied her.

The liquid felt good. She drifted off almost before the nurse helped her settle down again.

This time she was back in her home country, watching her baby grow up. Her husband had finished his studies, and was applying for a job. Nothing worthwhile ever came up. He was too qualified, not in the right specialization, or in the right field, but had no godfather to nudge the right people, the jobs were beneath his dignity as defined by his educational status. So she found a job, one that he directed her to. She did all the chores for the eight-member household before leaving for work in the morning and after coming back in the evening. And was humble and grateful because the in-laws took care of the baby. She didn't protest when they vied for the baby's allegiance, and ignored them when they gloated that the baby didn't care for her mother, the mother who rarely had a free moment during the baby's waking hours. She promised herself that she would win back the baby's love when her husband got his job and she had some free time. She tried. However, when the baby playfully tugged at her clothes, she snapped back, desperate to finish the piles of housework. She attempted to read at baby's bedtime, but fell asleep in exhaustion by the third sentence. And she kept waiting for the job that he was to get.

He kept looking for his job. In the meantime, he tried his hand at trading and small-time business. Just when one venture seemed promising, he got an incredible job. It took him all over the country. His flair to amuse people kept them busy within the social circles. He left that job and got an even better one. They had another baby. Her faith in him was rewarded. She prepared to enjoy motherhood, and was happy to let him take care of her.

And then the slump, a strike, a lockout, his pay suspended until the labor union reached a settlement. She started tutoring the neighborhood kids, at times holding the baby at her breast while doing math, or feeding the school-aged kid while she taught reading. And then there was the housework.

When the Canadian Immigration authorities responded to a query that was sent in years earlier, they jumped at the chance to start a new life. With the charm that only he could conjure, he wove dreams of a new beginning for her. He described a place where he would find a new job and they would build a new life for the children, where she would not fall asleep in exhaustion, instead of nurturing them. And she let him direct her dreams; her cheeks glowed, reflecting the fire within. There would be a life for them. She felt secure in his love and confident of his abilities.

The castle he had built in the air collapsed almost immediately on reaching Canada. The severe recession was sending most manufacturing south of the border. Almost every company needed "Canadian experience" before they would look at his résumé. Yet, how could you get the experience if you couldn't get your foot in the door! He lashed out with cynical jokes about the Canadian experience, the "Apply, apply, No reply" experience. He could predict the form letter response to the hundreds of applications he sent, without even opening the envelope. In the meantime, she found a job in her own field. She was afraid of driving ever since she had watched an old woman being crushed under a car. Overcoming her deep-rooted fear, she learned to drive.

She left the baby with unknown sitters, and agonized whether she was looked after properly. Stories about sexual abuse did not help her peace of mind. The poor child could not tell her whether or not she was fed properly. Used to constant care by loving adults, she was traumatized by the change of caregivers. Barely two, the girl would wake up screaming in the night, and then needed hours of cuddling before she could calm down. And her mother would get a few hours of sleep before the alarm went off. She laced herself with coffee to get through the workday, hoping she did not make a major mistake. The coffee would prevent her from falling asleep in the evening, and just as she drifted to sleep, the baby would start bawling again.

Her ten-year-old was initiated into Western society with cruelty that only middle-school children are capable of. Her accent was jeered at, her clothes snickered at, and the child withdrew into her shell, was reluctant to go to school, had no one to play with. The mother's heart bled at the sight of what her bright and effervescent child was reduced to. But the mother could find no solution, she could barely manage to feed the family, she had no strength to fight for her child. The spells of light-headedness, she attributed to lack of sleep.

One evening she was trying to amuse the baby and fell asleep in sheer exhaustion on the floor. The baby with all her two-year indignation, brought down her wooden blocks hard on her mother's face. She had no idea whether her husband noticed the bruises. He was so caught up in getting that better job, reading, applying, and getting into a deeper depression with every rejection. Finally, he tailored his résumé to appear as if he had minimum education and got an entry-level job. Each morning he wrestled with the indignity of semi-skilled work, reporting to superiors who were far less educated than he was.

At one point, a co-worker noticed as she struggled to maintain her balance when a wave of nausea swept her. "You really need to see a doctor," she remarked curtly.

Afraid of slipping up at the job, she went straight to the doctor's, hoping to get some potent vitamin supplement that would tide her over this ordeal. She had to fill in some routine papers for the nurse.

"When was your last period?"

She looked blankly at the lady. Assuming that the obviously new immigrant did not understand her, the nurse tried to phrase her question differently. She continued to stare blankly, noting that the nurse was dressed in pink. In her country the nurses always dressed in white. How would the patients know the difference between nurses and other patients? Her mind focused on trivial details, refusing to acknowledge the question. The nurse prodded her gently, and then gave her a calendar to help her. She didn't need a doctor to tell her.

She drove home, afraid, at the same time strangely elated. One for every country that she lived in. Both of her earlier pregnancies had culminated in a lot of happiness. It was a time of celebration, when she had felt a special closeness with her husband. Her mind had blanked out the preceding and succeeding events. All she could remember was the joy of the birth and the warmth of his affection. And some childish yearning within her convinced her that a repeat event would recapture the joy, the celebrations.

She tried to keep her secret, but the husband who did not notice bruises on her face immediately detected the excitement within her. The father, who did not appear to notice his older daughter's misery, wanted to know why his wife had come home by a different route. She could not keep track of her cycle, but he had a fair idea of how late she was. She could not lie when he confronted her. She tried to share her hopes, but his reaction — brutal, total — cut off her words. She had never seen him so fierce, so cold. It had to be taken care of, immediately.

He silenced her protests with a scathing remark: "You can't even handle one baby."

Angry, hot tears poured from her heart — the unfairness of it all. The years of slavery, the years of denial, the torture of trying to fulfil every role; breadwinner, housemaid, mother ... she recalled falling asleep while reading to her oldest, she remembered the bruises on her face, inflicted by the youngest. Her body gave up on her and she threw herself on the floor and cried for a long time. When the sobs subsided and the heaving stopped, she recalled with a start that she had to feed the family.

Rushing to the kitchen, she found her ten-year-old feeding a makeshift meal to the baby. That's when his remark cut something loose in her. She felt her flesh and blood shriveling. She saw her choices clearly, without being clouded by emotion. On the one hand were the children she could not take care of, and on the other she saw the promise of another life, a gift that she hadn't even asked for. She couldn't accept that gift without some help with her current responsibilities. She couldn't sacrifice the childhood of her ten-year-old to compensate for her inadequacy, and she could not count on his help. She shut her mind against the moral implications of the action she was considering, lest it weaken her resolve.

Her heart turned to stone. She called up the doctor, made the appointments and signed the papers. He drove her to the clinic without a word. She signed more papers and accepted the IV drugs without flinching. As the room darkened around her, she focused on the papers she signed. They seemed to float, turning to a dark shadow that lengthened and curled and crept up, ever so noiselessly, tightening and strangling ...

She sat up with a jolt, her mind clear. He came forward to assist with a smile on his lips. Coldly she cut him off. From now on she would stand on her own.

≪ ≪ ≪

Uhm-mah

Jin Lee

in the nape of my mother's neck, you can still see it
her dyed black silkworm hair, aged from fifty-five years of
    life, cannot hide it
even in her coffee colored eyes and on her wrinkled hands,
    it is there

the hardened balls of her feet reveal it
the gentleness of her voice sings it
the intensity in her face shouts it

like snowflakes gliding down from the cottonball clouds,
her beauty has a fragility that surrounds her
like a blissful breeze caressing one's face on an autumn
afternoon, her sweetness flows out to all that see her

but the secret vulnerability of her spirit is invisible to the
    naked eye
You see a crabbed, old, Asian woman,
lurching over her bowed legs to rob a penny from the
    Canadian ground
her foreign banter is acrid to you, leaving a bitter taste in
    your mouth
her mysterious scent offends you, evermore lingering in the air
but you do not taste the wonders she can create
you do not understand the power of just one word she utters
you cannot see the heartache she felt, being torn from her
    native land as a young bride
you cannot imagine the torture of having lost a father at the
    age of 9 to the Korean war

*This poem describes my mother and my admiration for the sacrifices
she has made and the hardships she has endured as a Korean woman.
"Uhm-mah" is the affectionate form of "mother" in Korean.*

Activated Pulses

Antara Chakraborty

You play with words
To find the right one
Go ahead, give it a try
You may be the scapegoat in the herds

They corner you
They poke 'n pinch
Testing your abilities
Accidentally you are new

Unseen on this side
Unfortunately wild
As a sunflower in rain forests
Urgently need to hide

Never did you dare
When those eyes gape
To run 'n go away
It's the way they stare

All you need to do now
Is turn your back 'n
Do what you want
Yet you never know how

There is the desire to run
It's expressed in every motion
You are the victim
They have the gun

You are scared to say
You have a life
A style
They hate your way

Build your movement
Master the trick
Show them who's right
Do be adamant

Verify you are tame
Yet hide your emotions
When time will come
Commence your game

First, play it false
Do it, your method
Care to live?
Activate the pulse

❧ ❧ ❧

Arman

Mehri Yalfani

A storm arrived and stole my footprint.
SOHRAB SEPEHRI

MINOO CAME OUT OF THE KITCHEN and looked at the window. She saw a winter sky with a black cloud, which deepened the darkness. She strolled towards the window to pull the curtains. Vahid, her husband, leaned on the sofa with his head on the back cushion, watching TV. Minoo stopped near the dining table. A few minutes ago, when she collected the supper's dishes, the TV was off. Vahid had been in Arman's room. Minoo had washed the dishes thinking about what happened since the afternoon. She was concerned about Arman, about how Vahid would talk to him and make him understand.

She stared at the darkness behind the window for a while. Her apartment was on the twenty-first floor in a high-rise at the edge of the city. Her view was a barren land and a grove, both dark in the night. A highway stretched far away, cars like ghosts passed through the darkness with two lit eyes and then were lost in the night.

Minoo turned to the TV. Two men — one with a dark complexion, thick eyebrows and a strong face, and the other with a sweat-red face and a stout body — were brutally assaulting a third man with fists and kicks. The third man was a punching bag, thrown this way and that. He was brought to the ground with a heavy fist. The black man hit his face. The camera showed a close-up. The victim's face was deformed. He groaned like an animal. Minoo turned from the TV to Vahid, who was absorbed by the film. An unwanted anger grasped her. The man's face falling on the ground was disgusting, but the two other men looked at him indifferently. Words stuck to Minoo's tongue. A cigarette

79

between Vahid's fingers, with its ashes close to falling. She wanted to say, "Be careful." She wanted to say, "Turn the TV off." She didn't. She just gazed at the TV, which was showing an empty street. The camera showed the two men climbing into a car, leaving the fallen man and driving away.

The cigarette's ashes fell on Vahid's black sock and spread like spit.

"Turn it off," Minoo said. But she didn't know if she meant the cigarette or the TV, or if Vahid didn't hear her, or heard her, but didn't care. Minoo looked outside the window at the darkness and lights glimmering far away. Vahid puffed his cigarette and kept the smoke in his chest and watched TV with its low voice. The only voice in the room.

The camera zoomed in again on the man. His face was out of shape and motionless. A stream of blood passed from his swollen lips. The street was dark.

"Turn it off," Minoo said loudly.

Vahid regained himself and looked at Minoo, but he didn't show any recognition. Minoo was angry. She didn't know if her anger was generated by violent film or Vahid's ignorant behavior, his sitting on the sofa. He was relaxing as if nothing had happened. She turned the TV off and stood by it. She stared at Vahid with his back to the deep dark. From where she stood, she couldn't see the car lights in the darkness. There was just a cloudy sky of cold weather. The wind howled like a savage wolf. A sudden fear rushed her — fear of the illusive, dark atmosphere outside the window.

Indifferent to her, Vahid turned the TV on again with the remote control. Two uniformed men put the fallen man, who might be dead or alive, on a stretcher and pushed him into an ambulance. In the next shot they carried him into a hospital. Police were there too. There was ignorance on all the faces. The same ignorance was on Vahid's face.

"Turn it off," she screamed.

Vahid looked at her, surprised. But still he ignored her. With a sharp movement, Minoo turned the TV off, took the remote control from Vahid's hand and tossed it toward the window — and the darkness. The remote hit the rocking chair, then the window, before it fell to the floor. Minoo shivered. The window could have broken, and cold and wind would have rushed into the room. She looked at Vahid, sat on the sofa and sobbed.

Vahid looked at her, wondering. He moved close to her, hugged her and said, "What's the matter? Why are you crying?"

Minoo wiped the tears from her face with her palm. She wondered why she had lost control. She tried to send the disturbed thoughts out of her mind, but she thought again about what had happened. She still couldn't believe it. She remembered their son Arman's face, his looking at her when she explained it to him.

He didn't want to see his father. He hid himself in his room, put the chair behind his door and sat on it to prevent his father from coming in. He wouldn't look his father in the eye, and didn't want to listen to him. She didn't know if he believed what his father had told him or not. He wasn't a child anymore. He was eleven years old. They had told him many times that he was a big man, and that he understood more than his age.

The room was full of silence. Minoo was exhausted and needed Vahid to talk to her. A vague question sat with her that she couldn't utter.

She looked at Vahid, who seemed indifferent. He lit another cigarette, puffed at it and sent the smoke out like a delicate cloud. Instead of the question which had occupied her mind, she asked, "Why did you lie to the child?"

Vahid didn't answer. He was busy with his own thoughts. Minoo asked louder, "I'm talking to you. Why did you lie to him?"

Without leaning on the sofa, Vahid bent his back and sat further away. For a while he stared at Minoo. She noticed shame in his eyes, shame she hadn't seen before. With Vahid it was always pride. Since the first time she had met him in the hospital — in a resident's uniform, with disheveled hair, as if he had just taken the surgery hat off his head and his sleeves rolled up — when he came out of the operating room. She was a nurse in the surgery department then. When they had met in the hallway, there was pride in his eyes. Pride and joy.

Then they got to know each other more. She had seen that pride and joy often in his eyes. And now, instead of pride there was shame. Shame in Vahid's eyes made her ashamed too. She wasn't innocent either. But she wanted Vahid to explain it for her. It was like a problem that should be solved. A problem that was with her for more than eight months, that was with both of them, and they knew that one day they should solve it. But they postponed it out of fear. They hoped the problem would solve itself. Now, not only had the problem not been solved, it had become more complicated.

Vahid stayed where he was with his bent back. Even his hands looked helpless — extinguishing the cigarette in an ashtray and then abandoned on his knees.

"Do you think it was my fault?" he asked.

"Whose was it then?" Minoo asked. "Was it me who deceived the child with his big lies?"

"No, it wasn't you. It was I. But, well, I didn't mean it."

"But you cheated the child."

"Yes, I did. But you aren't without fault either. You could have told him the truth. So you're guilty as well."

Minoo sat a little further and quieted. Yes, she was guilty as well. She could have told the truth. Why didn't she?

"Yes, you're guilty too," Vahid repeated. "You, too, never told Arman what work you are doing in the hospital."

"What are you talking about?" Minoo asked. "My fault is not as big as yours. You lied to him. You told him you're a surgeon. I didn't tell him anything."

"Did you tell him what you are doing at the hospital?"

"He never asked me."

"And if he asked, would you tell him?"

Minoo didn't answer. She asked herself, "Would I? Would I tell him the truth?"

82

Minoo had told her friends and acquaintances that she was working at the hospital, but she didn't say what she was doing. She had put her head on Vahid's shoulder, with a lump in her throat, had said, "We came here to have a better life. We thought we could progress here and find a place. And now, with this job! I'm an educated nurse. Why don't they accept me? Why should I do a job of an uneducated person?"

Vahid soothed her, "Wait for a while. It'll be okay. Let me pass my exams, get my license and work as a real surgeon then. But we didn't come here to be someone. When we were fleeing home, we just wanted to save our lives. We didn't think about these things. You know very well that we had to."

"But —"

"That's it. We should get on with it, and we have to try and do our best to get our real places." Vahid interrupted Minoo's thoughts. "Why? Tell me. Don't be shy. Why didn't you tell him the truth?"

"I couldn't. How could I tell him what I'm doing in the hospital? He thinks I'm a nurse. Well, I am. Am I not?"

"Yes, you are. Damn to whom denies it. I'm a surgeon, too. Am I not?"

"But here, you're not a surgeon. I mean, you tried to be, but you couldn't."

"What am I then? A butcher?"

Minoo looked at him and said nothing. But her eyes said, "Yes, you are a butcher, aren't you?"

Vahid continued, "Yes, I'm a butcher. I have to be a butcher. I had to win our bread."

Minoo put her hand on his knee and looked at him with sympathy.

"I didn't say you're a butcher."

"So what? Why are you so upset?"

"You know very well why I'm upset. What do we do with Arman?"

Vahid said impatiently, "I don't know what I'm going to do with him. You just accept that I had to."

83

"You had to lie to the child?"

"No, I had to be a butcher. I had no choices. You saw how much I tried. For five years, I had an ordeal. For five years I just dreamt about it and tortured myself about passing the exams. You witnessed that I had to accept any job for survival. I studied and I did any dirty volunteer job in the hospital with the hope that I could be a surgeon here, but it didn't work. So what could I do then? Hang myself? I had to live. So you'd better know that I like butchery. It's like surgery. Not much difference between them. The only difference is, with a human being, when you split his body, you want to put it together again. You should cure it, take a lump out of it and sew it again, or take a sick organ and replace it with a healthy one. But with butchery, it is a little different. When you have a carcass in your hands, you must cut it in pieces; take out its organs and sell them to people and make good money. You see, since I became a butcher, we have a better life."

He had a bitter smile on his face. He continued, "Yes, not too much difference. When I hold a butcher's knife in my hand and dissect a lamb or a cow, I remember the time I was in Pars hospital and opened a person's stomach."

Minoo stared at Vahid. She felt she didn't know him. A sneer on his face; his mustache disheveled, his thick black eyebrows, his big body, all became features of a butcher. She had gone several times to his butchery shop and had seen him with stained apron and plastic gloves, standing behind the counter with a big knife in his hand and chattering with the customers in a superior mood, bluffing about the meat he offered them. She sometimes tried to remember him in the Pars hospital, behind the operating table, only his eyes seen behind the surgery mask and a smile in them. Or when she went with Arman when the boy was five. Vahid in his white uniform of authority, talking to a nurse.

Over eight months, the man had changed slowly from a surgeon to a butcher. When he came home, the smell of fat and blood was on his whole body. He would go directly to the bathroom, wash himself and change his clothes. If he had a good day and good selling, he told some jokes he heard from his customers, and made Arman and her laugh. He told Arman about surgeries he did, feet he cut, hearts and livers he had taken out, and Arman believed that he was still a surgeon.

Arman would ask his mother where she worked, and she would say at the hospital. The child is happy with his parents' jobs, that both of them work at the hospital. But Minoo never had the guts to tell him what she was doing there.

Minoo stared at Vahid. She released herself from disturbing thoughts and said, "What should we do now? Now that he knows the truth, do you think he's lost his confidence in us? This afternoon, when he came home, you weren't home to see how he cried, saying, 'I won't believe you any more.'"

Vahid was quiet. Minoo said, "Ha? What do we do with him?"

"I don't know."

"How did he find out about it? Why did he come to your store? He didn't know where your store was. He didn't know you have a store."

"I don't know. That goddamn Kiumars brought him. Perhaps his father told him. He has seen my ad in the newspaper. You know, his father is a surgeon too. He too hasn't been able to pass the exams. He might have wanted revenge."

"Revenge? What revenge? Have you done something to him?"

"Last week, he came to my store. I told him, 'Man, you'd be better off to have a store in some other part of this city, not to forget you've been a surgeon. Instead of pizza delivery or driving a taxi, have a butchery shop.'" I told him that a butcher has a link with surgery that other jobs don't. I think he was offended and spoke to his son. His son is in the same school as Arman. Arman said that he called him a

85

liar in front of all the students and told them that his father wasn't a surgeon."

"Well, what if he doesn't want to go to school tomorrow?"

Vahid didn't answer.

"Ha? Have you thought about it? If he says, 'I'm not going to school,' what are we going to do?"

"Why wouldn't he go to school?"

"You said that Kiumars called him a liar and mocked him. What if other students mock him too? He was saying this evening, 'I'm not going to school any more.' Have you thought about it?"

"Yes, I did," Vahid said after a while.

"What?"

"I'll change his school. We'll move from this neighborhood. We'll move somewhere where no Iranis live, a place far from here. A place no one knows us."

"And will you tell him again that you're a surgeon?"

"No, it's no use to lie to him. He knows about my job. Why should I lie to him? Now, it's your turn to think about it."

"What do you mean?"

"I mean you should tell him what you are doing at the hospital."

"If he asks —"

"If he asks, you should tell him that you're not an educated nurse."

"Am I not?"

"No, you are not. You were, when I was a surgeon as well. But now, none of us are the same, what we were in those days. Now, we should accept what we are and our child should accept it too."

"Well, is it a question of the kind of job? The question is that we —"

"Yes, the question is that we rescued our lives, and now we are living and we …"

Minoo didn't hear the rest of Vahid's words. She was thinking, If they hadn't come. And then she yearned for the past. The days when Vahid and she met. She was a nurse, Vahid a resident in the surgery department.

She said, "I was thinking, if we hadn't come here, now you and I would be someone. Perhaps I would be head nurse of a department and you, a well-known surgeon."

Vahid looked at her in silence. It wasn't clear whether he was listening. Minoo, enthralled by her own thoughts, continued, "And we wouldn't have to lie to our Arman."

She waited for Vahid to say something. As he still was quiet, she asked, "What are you thinking about?"

"I was thinking, one forgets everything so quickly. You've forgotten that we had to flee. Forgotten that we had to abandon everything and flee at night. And if we hadn't, now we would either be in jail or underground or worse, repentant, not knowing ourselves."

Minoo said, with sadness in her words, "And perhaps we wouldn't have had the chance to have our Arman."

Then she rushed to the bathroom to wash her tears and swallow her lump, to prevent Vahid from noticing it.

❦ ❦ ❦

Arman is a male name and means a spiritual goal.

Winter Chill, A Silent Gratitude

Prabhjot Parmar

Huge cauldron in the restaurant kitchen
Sliding on the edge of the sink
Bare hands, slick with soap
Fingers callused, bleach-burnt
Scouring pads leaving permanent skin-peels.
No gloves allowed
The owner says,
"Pots will slip from your hands!"

Tired, sore back feels broken,
Out in the cold night
The 11 o'clock bus gets late.
Winter chill numbs shivering, tired body,
Somehow, mind has the ability to think
To look back.

She had the finest hands,
many said.
Vivacious and charming
Loved and loving
Raised with care, affection.
Parents, siblings and friends.
Carefree and free. Oh yes,
Free
Now chains
of orders
    of twelve-hour shifts
       of distrust
           of abuse
      of violation
    of imprisonment
of him.

The bus is here.
Thanks to the Transit Corporation
Warmth and comfort for a half hour at least
Huddling into the collar of the winter coat,
A Salvation Army buy,
Hurries out of the bus
Half hour bliss ends.
Runs to the house
Afraid to knock on the door.
Knocks.
He doesn't open.
Sleeping? Delaying? Punishing?
No
Only sadistic pleasure.

Polar wind chills her to the bone
Numbness overtakes
An eon of five minutes later the door opens
Barks of distrust follow,
"What took you so long?
Why are you so late?
Where were you?"
Three Ws gone wrong in the corridor of life.
Yanks her collar
Large-handed grip tightens
Choking
Thrusts her away.
Against the rickety coat hanger
Numbness dulls pain.
But
In the morning,
at the Long Term Care Aid facility,
she will feel it,
when lifting bulky beds, turning heavy bodies.

He curses.
She's silent. Learning lesson of two years of marriage
But, silence, too, enrages him.

Smack! On once peach-like cheek,
Splitting with excruciating pain
Unlike body
Face wasn't numb. It
was earlier huddled in winter coat's collar.
"WHO were you with?
Bitch."

Better life.
That's what she had thought
Looking out of the airplane.
The vast city, prosperity and happiness.
New life, hard work
Comfort.
Love.
That's what was to happen
Everyone had wished her luck.
Inner voice now yells,
"Leave him,
Go back!" No
Cannot go back.
Cannot tell them
Make them miserable too
Three younger sisters
Their marriages?
What will people say?
Parents will understand,
But
What will people say?

No tears
Frozen hand holds throbbing jaw
Tomorrow
Remember to
Keep face out of coat-collar
You won't need to clutch a numb cheek.

❧ ❧ ❧

Untitled Cycle of Prose Poems

Chrystyna Hnatiw

1.

A black chadra

softly draped

around her head

she boards

the last bus

from New York City

crumpled dollar bills

and an address

clutched in her hand

"Step up, damn it

no bills, change only

correct change only"

the driver barks

as if she understood

as if

there are more passengers

than three

we help her out

with the change

and when we plunge

into the darkness

the woman smiles

understanding nothing

about the anger

or our silence

staring intently

at the New Jersey address

warm only

in the cocoon

of her language

life however takes

a gentler turn

at the bus depot

my fellow passenger

gives a taxi driver

ten dollars,

the crumpled address

and with a simple

"Take care of her, eh"

heads towards

an all-night donut shop

and I return

to the empty bus,

the angry driver

I'm alone

but I feel warm

2.

By now

the rest of the world

has thrown away

its Christmas trees

cluttering

the backlanes of Winnipeg

with silver icicles

by now it's my Christmas

we bring to a Senior's Home

the fragrance

of freshly cut pines

seven, clean sanitary

immigrant women

a circle of lonely wheelchairs

as we carol

about birth and happiness

I notice Olga

standing apart

at the phone booth

just as last year

dialing the homes of her three sons

"You know what Canadian kids are like,

there must be a reason they're not here

I'm glad this isn't long distance"

she mumbles

it's only a ten-minute distance

to the homes

of her three boys

with their good jobs, nice houses.

I walk with her to her room

by now a haven

from the nostalgia of carols

her hand still moist

her quarter tired

she sits down quietly

placing her quarter

into a tin box

overflowing

with other dimes and other reasons

3.

You stood alone

under a parasol

of weeping willow rain

as migrant trains

set out for promised lands

you were a pioneer woman too

left behind

to the mercy of time

wondering when he would send for you

worrying

that your shawl was too frayed

too old for "Ameryka"

I would have bought you

the brightest, the warmest shawl

for that cold journey

now

in the silence

of Sundays

I weave for you

a wreath of sunlit tears.

4.

They told me that my accent

was too Ukrainian

the stoic, navy nuns

it was only my second month in Canada

and Lesia and I

could feel their steely eyes

when we skipped

quietly in Ukrainian

those eyes became warm only in the chapel

when we in unison recited

"Jesus I love you, Jesus I love you, Jesus I love you"

or

"Mother of Jesus pray for us sinners"

we kissed the bleeding heart of Jesus

fearing punishment in a small room

fearing a call to our parents

telling them

that we were not Canadianized enough

we yearned for that bell to ring

so that we could fly home

to the lilac bushes

to our homes that looked huge

where we could laugh and talk

and yes, skip in our language

❧ ❧ ❧

Still Running

Peggy Lee

how far
need I
run

running from my Britains
from British Columbia
to [post]-British colony
running from my difference
yet tongue-tied all the way

there you are chinky honger
here you are western bastard
    and woman
        educated
            sexualized
                politicized

adding to your list of treasons

threatening
beyond definition
or merely [re]define

running to my Chinas
from Chinese-Canadian
to Hong Kong Chinese
to Guangdong-ren

running to my sameness
yet the accent gives me away
marked by my difference
marked
  from outside
    from inside
      from all sides
        regardless
      shifting
  context

how far need I run

       🐚 🐚 🐚

Mothers

Sheela Haque

Mariam

SHE WALKS WITH A SLIGHT LIMP, which betrays her age, as she motions for me to sit down on the couch in the family room. Her waist-length hair is a long rainbow of black, gray and hennaed red, so characteristic of old South Asian women. She grunts softly as she ambles over to the tiny kitchen. The subdued blue color of her traditional thin material shalwaar and kameeze reveals the heaviness of her figure. She begins to boil tea for me, as is the custom for visitors. I rise from the couch and start to sit in one of the kitchen chairs. She protests, saying I should be comfortable. Politely, gently, I tell her that I am comfortable in the kitchen chair, and that I cannot hear her words when she is here and I am there. And to hear her words is why I came.

It is only because we are from the same background that she agrees to speak with me. I know that, although the elderly revel in telling their stories (and bore many by repeating them), few do so with people they barely know. But she feels alone, and I am the only one who will listen to her.

I am a psychiatrist. I do much listening. And I want to listen, and help her and her family. I have just come from talking with this woman's daughter, and now I am ready to hear her side.

She begins to slowly peel the vegetables and boil water for the evening meal as she talks:

"It is a disgrace, I tell my *bit-o*, Fatima, to watch these nonbelievers roaming around naked. In my country, we say these women who do not dress modestly are the fuel of hellfire. I have just recently arrived to the States, to care for this bastard child of my granddaughter, when it is brought forth from Allah's hands into ours. She is a shameful one, this Sadaf. Her mother has failed in her job of raising the child with Islamic mannerisms and values. In Pakistan, we do not let the parents stray so far from their duty; we do not let our children have such freedom that they commit these crimes. Our women are very important — more important than the men. There is this old proverb where I come from, 'A woman is like a string of beads; if broken once, it can be put together again, but can never be strung back the same way.' This is why we must protect them. This you know, eh?"

I nod to show her that I understand. But I know better than to divulge the fact that I do not agree. She will talk to me only because my age, modest dress and polite manners reveal me to be on her side. I smile in encouragement as she continues.

"But they do not listen to me anymore, these two women. I am just an old hag to them. They have grown to adopt non-Muslim habits. In my country, old women are treated with respect, and when we give advice, the listeners take it. They do not brush it aside like it means nothing, like this Sadaf does. They do not make believe that they are listening and then go and do whatever they want to, as my daughter Fatima does."

She has finished peeling and washing the vegetables. Now slowly, with an effort, her wrinkled, veiny hands trembling, she picks up the pile of peels on the newspaper and transfers it to the garbage. The water for the rice has begun to boil. She dumps the rice into the enormous pot before continuing.

"They do whatever they wish. It is almost a good thing that they have not chosen to live in Pakistan because these corrupt, modern views they hold would not be tolerated there. These *haraam* actions would surely be punished. Fatima, she has done a disgraceful thing, divorcing her husband as she did. And *oay*, she gives no good reason for this shameful act. We do not know why she has done it, and so she has had to raise her children with no assistance from anyone. His family will not help her and I will not help her.

No, I will not help her any more than my nature will allow me. There is a saying in my country, which is similar to this one here that goes 'One has unmade their bed, and now they must lie in it.'"

She chuckles, weakly coughing. She reminds me of my old aunt, who constantly tries to be cool by using American phrases and ends up sounding even more foreign than before. I turn my attention to this old woman, who peels and cleans the vegetables as she speaks.

"No, it was not my place to help her. But now she has begged me to come, and I am a mother. I cannot resist the pleas of my child. And this child of hers, Sadaf, *oh us ka kya karoon, win to ban gayee-guzree hai*, she is even worse. She has committed a sin so vile that she will burn one day for her passions. She is a wild one, and has no shame. Can you believe, she is with child and the father is a non-Muslim!"

She looks to me in disbelief, obviously hoping I will jump in and agree with her. I am here to only listen, and not talk, even if we are from the same background. I wonder if her daughter has explained this to her. Then I ask her to elaborate.

"May Allah forgive her, for I surely cannot. But these two, they think their lives are trying, but they have not ever experienced real pain and suffering. They do not know what it feels like to work so hard that you feel your limbs so heavy, like they will fall off. But I have known these things. I have felt these things."

She squints at me, as if sizing me up. She finally says, "I will tell you my story, Shama, because I feel that you are wise, and I can trust you. Come."

By now she has finished cooking the vegetables and rice that will be the evening meal. She covers them with old yellowed plates to keep them warm. Then she shuffles out of the kitchen, her *hijab* trailing after her. I follow her out of the kitchen, glad that her job for the day is done. She had cleaned the house earlier, and it is as spotless as the cramped little place can be. She settles down on one of the lopsided blue couches in the family room and motions me to sit in the one opposite her. Then she starts talking again.

"This is my story. It begins almost sixty years ago. Although we were very poor, my family had the most respect in our village because we were the only Sayeds, not only in our village, but in the neighboring one also. We carry the blood of Prophet Muhammad *(Sulla la a lay hee wa sullan)* in our veins. At that time, Pakistan was not there; it was all India. And we all had to struggle and survive together, Muslims and Hindus, under one country, ruled by the British. It was not easy. There were many fights and civil wars throughout the land. The Hindus believed that since this was first their land, we should bow to their laws and customs. They were enraged when we would slaughter cows for food. But we needed to eat, and so did what was necessary to survive.

"Life was very harsh. My father would wake up every morning and plow the fields until the sun set. Still there was not enough food to go around. During a good season the rain would come and provide enough food. But the rain was not always a good thing; it would melt down our mud house and create many dirty puddles. It made it hard to remain clean. For the boys, it was not a problem, but we women were different. For these reasons and others that I will not mention. That is why, when he was offered a way to feed and clothe one of us, my father took it. I do not like the choice he made, but I did abide by it, for it was my duty. I was to be married … yes, to a young boy of five."

I gasped in surprise. I had never heard of this before. She noticed the look of shock on my face and responded to it. "It sounds very strange, I understand. A fifteen-year-old girl marrying a child, but so it was. My father-in-law, Abu Hamza, was an old, old man. His wife had died, leaving him with two young boys. He had not the means to work in the fields and take care of them. With no relatives the only choice was marriage. But he could not just bring in a woman to mind his house, for that would be shameful and lecherous in the eyes of the village — an old man with an unmarried girl living with him! And for him to marry a young girl would also have been very indecent. His only option was to marry off his eldest son. I was chosen over my sisters because my skill in the house was more than theirs. When I was told the news, I did not cry until my father had left the room. He did not permit tears, for he thought them a sign of weakness. So I went, alone and scared, into a new village to care for this family. Time went by, and soon I began to tire of the long days. My new father did not permit me to converse with the other women in the village, for he feared some secret of my family would come out and he would be disgraced. Many times I told him that my family has no dishonorable secrets, but he would not believe me. Every night I cried, from the pain of my body and the loneliness in my heart.

"At this time malaria was one of the many diseases common to the people. I was very susceptible to it, and was taken ill by it on numerous occasions in the six years I lived with Abu Hamza. For weeks on end I would remain sick, in bed, while Abu Hamza lost time in the fields to tend to me and the boys. I became more of a burden than a help, and one night I heard him speaking of how he wanted to find a wife for his other boy because I could not do the job right. He could not let me go, for divorce is not a respectable thing. I knew that I could not stay in that home any longer. Although I had great fondness for the children, I would not become part of the charity package this new *aurat* would have to take on. So later that night, in a fit, I escaped to a nearby village and lived hidden with a family who took me in as a maidservant. In exchange for my service, they would keep my secret and provide me a husband. A year later, I was wedded to a respectable man. With him I raised four children. I never saw my family after that, because they would surely send me back to Abu Hamza. Now I am here to care for another child, as that is all I have done in my life. *Hai meri Allah!* I am so tired."

As she finishes, she rests her head back against the couch. I wait for a few seconds, and then tell her that it is time for me to leave. She starts to wearily rise to lead me out, but I remind her that I must talk to her granddaughter. She nods, distracted. I tell her that she should lie down on the couch and rest. She agrees, and so I help her. As she closes her eyes and I pack up my things, I think about how there is something very endearing about her. A few minutes later, the still silence is replaced with the peaceful sound of her soft snoring, and I head for Sadaf's room.

Fatima

MARIAM'S DAUGHTER IS a middle-aged woman with short, slightly graying hair. She is the one who contacted me to help her with her family problems. Unlike some South Asians, she does not believe that we psychiatrists are silly quacks, helping people with what they should be able to do on their own. Her slumped shoulders only hint at the weight she must carry. It is now lunchtime and the doctor's office has closed. She had asked me to come to where she works and, had she been a real client and not a friend of a friend who was receiving my services for free, I would not have agreed. But I know that I must meet all three women and hear their different versions of the situation before I begin counseling. Fatima plops down on the brown chair and opens her lunch as she begins, motioning me to also eat.

"I do not know what to do about this shameful problem. I have brought my mother here to take care of the baby if Sadaf decides to have it."

She looks up at me with big eyes and asks, "You will meet Sadaf after this, right?" I calmly reassure her that I will, and ask her to tell me how she feels about bringing her mother to America. She concentrates on her cheese sandwich as she talks, as if she's going to dissect it instead of eat it.

"She is an old woman, my mother, about eighty-five,

108

and I feel very guilty for asking her to come here to take care of my two babies. I should be the one taking care of her in her old age, not the other way round. She does not really know her exact age. This new baby's birth date will not be forgotten though. We will celebrate it every year, whether Sadaf keeps the child or not."

Now she begins to talk with some passion. It surprises me slightly, but I just listen to her.

"We must celebrate it, to remember that this creature exists, even if he or she is not with us, because this child will be somewhere in this world. It will not be up in heaven with the many babies killed every year before they're even allowed to breathe the breath of life. Oh no, abortion is out of the question in this case. It is against our beliefs. No, she will surely not have an abortion. It is merely a case of keeping the baby or giving it away for adoption. She must never do what I did as a young girl."

I look at her questioningly, and she hesitates. I encourage her, and she continues, a little frightened.

"It all began in Pakistan in the late sixties. There was much chaos then, as there is now. You didn't grow up there, so you don't know what it was like. Your parents may remember a bit. The clashes between the Hindus and us escalated. Vandalism of the mosques by Hindus, and their temples by us, was not an uncommon occurrence. I knew of a band of boys from my village, when their so-called religious patriotism reached a peak, who would take a cow to one of the Hindu villages, slaughter it and run. And similarly, although it was abhorred in their religion, Hindus would bring swine into our village and do the same. The more dangerous types of patriotism took the form of violence, rape in particular. Hindu men would rape young Muslim girls, and vice versa. I don't understand why this religious ferocity was so important that our men would rape, *rape*, young Hindu girls. This is a terrible thing in Islam, yet they would do exactly that in the name of Islam."

She paused. These were things that I had heard about.

I tell her this, and ask her to go on. She takes a deep breath before continuing.

"I was a victim of these rapes. That is why I am here in America. My family could not let me have the baby there, unmarried. So I was quickly married off to a family friend, Adeen, who was coming to America to do his residency in medicine. He assumed the baby was his, conceived on our wedding night. It is he who convinced me to have an abortion once we arrived in the States. I was young, naïve. I had absolutely no knowledge of the outside world, coming from a tiny village in Punjab. I knew that it was a wrong thing to do, but I was alone, far from my family, with no friends. I was with this worldly, handsome, kind man. I wanted to be the best wife I could be for him. I believe it was partly because of the guilt I felt for hiding this enormous secret from him, and partly because I would've tried to be a good wife with any man I married. And he wanted me to do this one thing for him, so that our futures would not be destroyed by such a responsibility that neither of us was ready for.

"So I crumbled under the pressure. I told my family that I had a miscarriage. They said nothing, but were very relieved. I never spoke of this to either my family or my husband after it was over. You kind of think that it is in the past. But, although it was a bastard child, I will never forget. Every year on what would have been this child's birth and what was its death, I remember and I think about it. I cannot do these things openly, so I mourn in my mind. They are the only days I allow myself to cry for this child. Adeen did not understand that I cry over the emptiness of what should have been there. He knows I blame him for the abortion and the resulting depression I feel because of it. He would tell me to focus on the two children that I do have. But how can one simply forget such a loss? How could I forget the rape that went with it? Maybe that's why I divorced him. Because he could so easily forget about the child.

"But that is only part of the reason. Living in the States in the early seventies with the resurgence of the women's movement was an extraordinary thing. I became fascinated with it. This was not a hard thing, for I know of many Muslim women who came to the States at that time and were similarly fascinated. With this, some left Islam altogether, unable to reconcile the demands of Islam with the feelings in their hearts. But I was able to incorporate feminism into my view of Islam. But Adeen couldn't understand these ideas. All he saw was that I was there to clean his house and bear his children. When the children started kindergarten and I wanted to start working, he was appalled. When I began to make friends with both Muslims and non-Muslims, he would only allow me to see my Muslim friends, and that, when he visited their husbands. He would object when I would allow Sadaf to play with those GI Joe toys and encourage Ahmad to play with his sister's Barbie dolls.

"It hasn't even been a whole year yet. It seems like I lived a whole different life when I was with him. No matter how much I try to explain to my mother why I divorced him, she does not understand. When I tell her we were not in love, she thinks it's because I didn't try hard enough to please him. When I tell her we had nothing in common, and were living like two people sharing a house, she says I should not have done things and gone places without him. He is gone now and that is all that matters.

"Oh, but we are here to talk about Sadaf, my little oyster. She has fallen into a similar trap as mine. But for her it is much worse because she initiated this corruption. It was not rape; this was her fault. She fell in love with a non-Muslim. She went behind my back and dated, dated him. She had sexual relations with him. And she is generally a very good musalimina. What a shock! Oh my God, I was so angry when I found out. I still am, but how long can one be angry for? I must get over it and help her now. I don't understand why she has done this to me! It is a shame to our good family name. She tells me that it was a mistake, that they were careful to use protection, so she shouldn't have got pregnant. But as my mother would always say, he who cannot dance, blames the courtyard for being crooked. Sadaf shouldn't have been doing something in which she would need to be careful in the first place."

She puts her head on the desk before continuing. She looks so forlorn, that I want to tell her that it will all be okay. But I just let her talk.

"All of her life I tried so hard to raise her into a good Muslim girl, as I was raised. But it is very hard in this non-Muslim society to raise good Muslims. Very hard. Sadaf tells me of the Muslim girls in her high school, and how some of them lie to their parents. They do not realize that although their parents do not see what they do, Allah sees everything, for he is the All-Knowing, All-Present. I am glad my daughter does not do this.

"She has not yet made a decision, but I think she will have the baby. I was so proud of her, she was going to go to Yale. She would have been the first woman in my family to go to college. But now she has responsibilities. Surely she cannot go. No, she cannot go."

As Fatima speaks, she lets out a long sigh. She tells me that her lunch break is over. Neither of us has eaten much of our food. She stands up and stretches her work-stiffened body. I too stand up and get ready to leave. I tell her that I will talk to her daughter, and then we will be able to begin family therapy. As I leave, I see her sit down and lean back in the chair, shutting her eyes for a moment before getting up to change the door sign from "closed" to "open."

Sadaf

SHE IS A TALL GIRL OF SEVENTEEN, with shoulder-length hair and green eyes that are a rarity for South Asians. She tells me she will not have much time to talk. She paces back and forth in her room of soft purples and blues. I glance around and notice the many posters and pictures of friends that

112

cover the walls. I can't even see the floor because of all of the clothes, magazines and CDs. She is clearly anxious. I ask her what the problem is.

"Ryan is on his way over to take me to have an abortion. My mother doesn't suspect. I got into Yale, for God's sake, and she expects me to give that up for the baby. Isn't that crazy, Shama? She should understand, though. Growing up, all I heard was 'You can do anything you set your mind to. It doesn't matter if you're a girl. You can do anything your brother can, maybe more.' My mother is a weird combination of modern American views and traditional Pakistani views.

"Another thing she always told me is to live my life for myself and no one else. She is always telling me about my grandmother — how she lived her life for everyone but herself. I expected her to be loving and sweet, like the grandmothers you see on TV, but she's not. Taking care of all those people but herself must have made her pretty bitter. She's convinced I'm going to hell for what I've done. But I want to focus on this lifetime and not be so caught up in the next one.

"Not missing out on this life means not missing out on medical school. Right now my life is more important than this baby's. Adoption is out of the question. If I wanted to keep this baby, I would raise it myself instead of giving it to some rich couple who could never love it as I could. Besides, how many people are looking to adopt a South Asian baby, anyway?"

I ask her if she's told other people about the baby, more specifically, her father.

"No, I haven't told him yet. My brother knows, and the baby's father, Ryan, but not my father. I don't think I can deal with that. He's very religious. I mean, I'm religious too, but in a different way. I see religion more as spirituality. I don't need to complete certain actions like praying or fasting to know that I'm a good Muslim. My one 'bad' deed is having a relationship with Ryan.

"My brother took the news pretty hard. We're pretty close, even in our ages, but Ahmad wouldn't talk to me for a week. I think just the idea that I was capable of having sex shocked the hell out of him. Once he got over that, he could deal. He's more religious than I am, so the first thing he did when he was talking to me was make me pray with him to God for forgiveness. The next thing he did was beat up Ryan.

"My father had this saying to explain why my brother and I had different rules: 'A woman is like a precious jewel, and accordingly, she must be kept under strict security and guarded so that she is not stolen when she shines the brightest.' So Ahmad's always played the protective big brother role. But he knows me better than my mom. He has tried to talk me out of the abortion, but he'll live with it.

"My mom, though, will cry, cry, cry. She's worried about our Muslim identity slipping away with each generation. She's also going to feel like she's failed as a parent. She already feels that way, especially when it comes to me. Grandma doesn't help the situation by constantly harping. She'll probably croak when she hears the news. Ryan should be here by now."

She peers out the window, looking for the familiar red Honda. Seeing nothing, she sits back down on her twin-sized bed. I ask her if she wants me to come along too. She says no, but that she might be calling me later, after she tells Fatima about the abortion.

"I feel so guilty about Mom. I don't want to hurt her, but what can I do? We have this incredible connection and I feel like it's slowly being pulled apart, like stretching taffy until it's two separate piece —"

Sadaf jumps up and grabs her purse at the sound of a car horn. I quickly gather up my things and we leave the house, being careful on the way out not to wake her sleeping grandmother in the family room.

❧ ❧ ❧

114

Curry Brown Lives

Amal Rana

Shall i compare you to curry?
hot and spicy
so many variations of
flavor
texture
smell
feel
color
yes color
the color of curry
burnt curry?
hot curry?
mild curry?
kashmiri curry?
brown curry
with golden hues
red hues
rich and smooth
like me
like you
full of surprises
burning the tongues
of those who
taste us
shocking them
with
unexpected
fire
something
to sample
to taste
novelties from a far-off place

something
to savor
to gasp at
whisper about
something
to show off
to talk about
at dinner
with other white women
something
to temper down
make mild
take away
some of the
heat
the
masala
make us more
acceptable
for western tongues
more civilized/colonized
yet still
fashionably exotic
and of course
ethnic
a real taste of
South Asia
a real glimpse
into
our curry brown lives

Oh Canada

Peggy Lee

Oh Canada

My home on Native Land

True patriot love you can't command from me

With my own eyes, I see my truth

Reserves on Native land

From far and wide

    Oh Canada

    "Let's blame minorities!"

"Strained services ... stealing all our jobs!"

    Oh Canada, here's my re-a-li-ty

    Why blame yourself,

    it's easy to blame me.

            ❦ ❦ ❦

You Go to Him

Fatima Correia

I GREW UP HEARING THE STORIES my mother told about her friends, family and the community she knew in Portugal before immigrating. Somehow she conveyed more through her vocal and facial/body expressions than through the actual content; an emotional or intuitive meaning that is difficult for me to describe. It was through these tales that I could develop some understanding of my parents' life before they came to Canada, and what it meant to have a Portuguese identity. They evoked in me a variety of images, thoughts and feelings that provided the backdrop for my eventual travel to Portugal as a young adult. I guess in some ways both my parents, like many others, are oral historians, their stories and jokes well ripened by the constant retelling and reshaping.

When I asked my mother if she was willing to be interviewed, she agreed to do it without hesitation. In fact, she seemed quite pleased. We arranged an interview time (after 11 p.m., my time, when I can get the cheap long-distance rate). That night arrives, and I am lying down on my bed with a tape recorder close to the phone, checking if the tape machine is working. On the bed, I have a pen and some sheets of paper.

Both my parents grew up in small farming villages in a Portuguese province that is largely agricultural. Although Portugal has a long history as colonizers in continents such as Africa, South America and Asia, it is difficult to articulate how that wealth trickled down and advanced the peasant class in Portugal, to which my parents belonged. Even so, Portugal, as a whole, clearly gained much from being an imperial power at the expense of indigenous peoples' lives, cultures and resources. I wonder now, how that climate of opportunism influenced the decision my father made to leave the country and, ultimately, the decision my mother made to follow him. The prevailing religious faith in Portugal continues to be Catholicism, which still exerts considerable moral and political influence. Both my parents grew up Catholic and hold fairly traditional views on a variety of issues. My mother is the younger of two in her family, and my father is third in a sibling line of seven.

I ask my mother how she came to make the decision to leave Portugal. She responds:

> *Dad [your father] was working at the airport [as a policeman]. And he used to see people coming from America and Canada; they had money and all that stuff. So Dad was quite enthusiastic about immigrating to Canada. So once we had a chance of coming, we discussed it, both of us, and I said, "Well you can go, but I would never go."*
>
> *So he said, "Okay, I'll go for a couple of years and make some money, and then I'll come back. And if I need to make some more money, I'll go work there in the summers and come and stay in the winters."*
>
> *So I [decided] I would go back to my mother. So Dad came — he gave up his job to go to Canada. Well, once that I was there [in Portugal] and you were born, I missed Dad again and, you know, I was feeling sorry for him, he couldn't see his baby and all that stuff. [I was] always telling him that I would never come. This first letter I got from him he was complaining that he had to wash his clothes, and do his own cooking and all. I felt sorry for him. So after you were born, it was worse. He said, "If I knew how the life was in Canada, I would never have come all by myself."*

At this point we clarify that my mother was six months pregnant when my father left. She continues:

> *The hardest part was leaving my mom. I was crying for Dad, and Grandma was without my father for six years when he was*

120

in Argentina. So she knew how hard it was. She said, "Better go, your place is with your husband — you better go to him." So I decided to come, but with the idea of being here for two or three years, make some money and then go back. You know, thirteen months after I came, [your sister] came along, and then the money, you know, we didn't make as much money as we thought. And the more we make, the more we want to have. Harder to go back [chuckles].

And then you started going to school, and we bought a place because we wanted a place for ourselves. I started working and making friends and things like that. I wanted to go back very badly too, but once that you started in school, and started your life here — it was so hard for me to leave my home country and come to a strange country, and, uh, everything being so different, so hard. We didn't want you to go through what we went through. You know, little by little, and Grandma died, and then I didn't want to go back.

I was hundred per cent sure before we went back [to Portugal] you know I thought that we could go back. But when we went back the first time, everything was so different. Where the children are is where we like to stay.

This is my mother's story. The dream to leave and have a more prosperous life wasn't hers, but rather my father's. She resisted. She was caught in a double bind; wanting neither to live apart from her husband nor leave her mother. I wonder also if, after having given birth, she feared living a life as a single parent, as her mother had done before her for six years. Although she clearly states how she missed my father, it is significant that she tells the story largely from the perspective of his needs. That my mother finds it difficult to voice her own desires, thoughts and feelings except through my father's viewpoint reflects women's historical domination and silencing in patriarchal societies.

My mother also talks about not wanting to re-impose her own trauma on her children by taking us to Portugal. It seems that my grandmother had a similar struggle because she encouraged my mother to leave, although it was painful for her to do so. The dilemma for both my mother and grandmother was how to make a decision, taking into account everyone's needs and negotiating the turmoil that decision may elicit. It seems that, for my mother, her home country and the complex emotional meanings and representations it evokes are intimately linked with her love for her mother. When my grandmother died, she was not able to go back for many years and face the emptiness and the feelings it aroused. The conflicted feelings raised in not wanting to leave her mother is evident when she states:

We couldn't even say good-bye. It's even hard to think about it.

I can hear in my mother's voice how painful this loss is for her. Hearing how conflicted she still feels allows me to understand how I, too, have a tremendous fear of loss and, as a result, cope poorly with separation.

Later in the interview, I ask my mother to tell me what it was like to come to a strange country.

When I arrived — when I saw your father [pause] after seven months, I hardly recognized him. He had lost so much weight. And he was so slim that I said, "What happened to you?"

He said, "I've been working hard."

Back home, it wasn't very hard work in those days when everything was nice and quiet. He would work six hours and rest eighteen. So you know he had a really easy life. He came [to Canada], he worked so hard that he lost all that weight and the food wasn't very good that he was cooking.

I should clarify that my father was working as a farm laborer for people who owned fruit orchards. My mother goes on to talk about an English couple my father was working for and how they were very helpful, in fact, "exceptional" as she put it. She states:

She wanted me to learn English. Before I came, [my nephew] said, "Tia [aunt], you should learn English."

I said, "I don't need it. When I get there, you know, Tio [uncle] will do all the shopping." I was planning to just be the lady of the house. Once I got here and I saw our house, that little cabin, you know it wasn't what I expected.

I ask, "Didn't Dad prepare you for that?" She responds:

He said, "One thing that you are really going to miss is the house." But you know I never expected it to be like that. Small, but you know.

I find it interesting that my mother was so dismayed and shocked. There is an illusion of abundant prosperity in North America (even more so at that time), which feeds into the "land of opportunity" immigrant dream. Perhaps she was also drawn to some kind of romantic heterosexual myth. As well, my father apparently didn't want to disenchant my mother. However, her hopes were quickly dismantled. She tells me:

And then when I started helping Dad, the first thing that he was doing was thinning the peaches. I picked you up and I went to the place where he was thinning. And I felt so hot I got a sunstroke. But then you know I got used to it and it was okay. The hardest, you know, was if anybody came and knocked on the door. I was so scared of anybody coming and knocking at the door. I'd just say, "No speak English, no speak." I wanted to get rid of people, you know. Life was so different. Back home, you know, I used to know people, and everybody was treating me well. Here I wanted to be underground.

I am struck by this metaphor of being underground and how it speaks to her homesickness, isolation and depression in making this transition. When I ask her to tell me some of the things that made it better, she talks about support from

123

friends, getting lifts, learning English and attending night school. There was also an organization through the Catholic Church that helped new immigrants. Eventually, she joined the choir. Despite these adaptations, my mother says, she was "always thinking of going back." I ask her to describe Grandmother for me.

> *Grandma. She was a saint. She was a very, very unselfish person. I think because she wished to have a daughter for so many years, and then when I came along, I was spoiled a lot. But I had a lot of respect for the elder people, my uncle, Grandma, Tio, I still have. I was spoiled, but I think at the same time I was humble. Because if they said, Don't do this, I wouldn't. I was spoiled, but didn't rebel.*

She acknowledges that she can't think of any bad points about her mother. When I ask about my grandfather, she tells me that she was also "very close" to him, as she was to her only brother. The idea of being good and doing as she is told is important for my mother. Perhaps my mother's idealized view of her parents is related to guilt at not continuing to be the obedient daughter by staying in Portugal. Or, perhaps, her belief in and deference to authority constrained her and immigrating was one way for her to rebel and not be so obedient.

My mother then begins to talk about her fear of coming to a new country:

> *I was even overprotecting you when I came, on my way here. Before I left I said to Tio, "I'm not scared of anything, I'm just scared of the baby, if anything will happen to her." He said, "Don't worry." Because, you know, books that I had read from America, about stealing babies and things like that. I was so scared. And he said, "Don't be crazy, they only steal babies from the rich people, [laughs] you don't have a penny."*

What I find interesting here is that my mother describes

her fear of any harm being inflicted on her child and she discounts or denies any fear that she herself may be hurt. This tendency to put her own needs aside and focus on those of her child was not uncommon with my mother, and it reflects the general devaluing of mothers in cultures steeped in sexism. For my mother, overprotecting her children and focusing on the needs of others may have been one way for her to cope with her own insecurities or fears, which she was not encouraged to express in a more direct fashion. I am reminded of the importance of paying attention to the indirect and veiled ways in which women and other oppressed groups may communicate their experiences.

When I was growing up, my mother and I fought many battles regarding what I was permitted to do outside the home. As an adult, I began to understand that the intensity of these conflicts was partly due to my mother's fears that her children could be adversely affected by a culture of which she had little understanding. Also interesting, in my opinion, is how my mother generally complied with her parents' wishes, whereas, a generation later, I resisted and challenged some of her rules.

My mother goes on to talk about how it was a blessing when her niece immigrated to Canada and lived with us, because the two had been close in Portugal. I ask my mother what she thinks things would have been like if she herself had not left. She answers:

I didn't think about it. Sometimes in the first year, I would get so tired and upset, I would say, "If [only] you [had] stayed," because we had enough for us with Dad's wages and the property that we had, you know. We would have potatoes and beans and all the vegetables and things like that. We wouldn't suffer. Not very extravagant. But we would have enough for ourselves. And I used to blame him. And then, you know, after I was blaming him, I started feeling guilty too because to come here, he had to give up his job. So once he couldn't go back, you know, I started to realize I shouldn't tell him that, because he was feeling sorry sometimes that he came and thinking back about it. So I stopped myself. Wherever we are, we all have our cross.

This conflict was difficult for my mother to resolve and she appears to have silenced herself in order not to burden my father. It seems that she did not understand my father's insistence and drive. When I question her about this, she states that his motivation was grounded in hearing about the positive immigrant experience, the money, and his unhappiness with his work as a policeman. When I ask about her motivation, she responds:

I remember when I came, I only brought two sets of sheets and blankets and a very, very thin bedspread. Because I was thinking I would come and in a few years go back. It was very hard, but it was hard for Dad too. Because he was working very hard. And Dad never told me to put more hours in or pressed me to work.

Evident in my mother's story is the importance of my father's drive to "make it" in the new country, the hardship this entailed for him and how she supported him, despite her own ambivalence. When I further ask about why my father's experience was so different from hers, she states:

Dad was away from his family for so many years. And Dad's family is not so close together as my family — I don't know, I don't know the reason. Besides, he was a man, he would put on his eight or ten hours, and I was home, you know, just looking at the four walls.

I wonder if, at one time, she questioned why the separation was so difficult for her. Here her experience of disconnection — different from that of my father, who was pursuing his dream — reveals her vulnerability and isolation. She tells me more about her mother:

126

She lost her memory the last year of her life. And when she took sick, [her voice gets very soft] I said, "I'll go."

But Tio said, "Well, if you come, you have to plan to stay for a while." And I couldn't because you were already in school. And Tio said, "If you just come for a few weeks and then go, better not to come."

I didn't go, but I regretted it. The worst part was that she wanted to have a daughter to take care of her in her last days, and I left her. She always said, "You go, you go to him." But she never thought that I wouldn't go back. I never sent for my things while she was alive. Only after she was gone did I ask Tio to send my stuff.

My mother starts to cry as she tells me that she doesn't want to talk about it. Her voice becomes almost inaudible. I start to cry too, and tell her that she needed to say good-bye to her mother when she left Portugal. She states:

No, I didn't. And she didn't. She even said, "I don't want to. I don't want to. You go."

When I suggest that maybe she did not return when her mother was alive because she was afraid she would never leave again, she replies:

Oh, if I went back and I had taken you I wouldn't come back. For sure.

My mother's sadness and guilt about leaving her mother and never returning or saying good-bye continues to trouble her. As a child, I never knew my grandmother, but I did know that my mother seemed caught, even trapped, between meeting the conflicting needs of her two families living apart. I knew she could not leave us. My mother had many fears of how her daughters would be changed by a rather hostile Canadian environment. She may have also

127

been afraid to say good-bye, even temporarily, to her daughters and re-experience any feelings of loss. Perhaps even more frightening for my mother was that she did not want to experience saying good-bye to my grandmother, and her home and culture.

Each time one of her three daughters left home my mother experienced a deeply painful process; it may have rekindled her old grief. In my relationship with her, I struggle to empathize with her fears of my growing distance because of education and acculturation. The distance reflects our different values, priorities and life goals. Maintaining connection requires a tremendous amount of effort on both our parts. In a way, this narrative is a bridge that allows us to maintain a connection between the different worlds we inhabit.

Interviewing my mother and transcribing the tape stirred up feelings of sadness and pain. It helped me become more understanding of my mother's struggles. The fact that my mother likes her story and wants to see it in print is my reward, a healing gift. I encourage other women who have not yet done so to write about their mothers and hope that mother-daughter narratives will be told and retold in a multitude of distinct voices, of which this story is simply one.

※ ※ ※

My-Lady-In-The-Cage

Laurie Anne Whitt

for Maria Perrone,
a portrait following electro-shock

i

Your wig has slipped ever so slightly.

A smile half-set
uneasy in its face
scarcely tries to begin
and five baby-fine hairs
go grayly escaping at the nape

Swaying, somewhat askew
you watch me
from all your dark
corners,
clothes
five layers deep and
waiting

Once dispossessed (they say) twice wary.

Rigid with cure and eased
of history
you settle
solemnly rebuking sight:
a giant oak uprooted

ii

Nothing can be erased:
not the swollen moons
of suspicion where
your eyes loom indelibly
glowing from the dark
nor the ornate frames
and broad floral patterns
of your baroque, stubbornly
Sicilianate tastes

iii

I can neither share nor end your confinement.

only pace
from a discrete distance
at its beginnings
where the passage of light
is obstructed & the haunted
eye trapped:
a clouded, paper-thin
impenetrability

where a voice is raised
to your hushed dignity
my lady
caged in words

✄ ✄ ✄

130

My Great Trek

Anonymous

THE YEAR WAS 1985 in Johannesburg, South Africa, and violence was at its peak. Apartheid was becoming intolerable and the people were starting to revolt. We had been thinking of migrating to the US for some time because part of my father-in-law's family was there already. In South Africa, my family was quite orthodox. A woman's place was at home and she did what her husband and in-laws wanted. We lived in the heart of the city, where it was becoming increasingly dangerous. The children were driven to school and back. Once home, they were locked indoors. But we also owned six theaters and other properties. We were pretty well off and didn't really feel like leaving the country and starting over.

When I realized that my five children didn't have equal opportunity to excel, I knew sooner or later we would have to move. My children went to private schools, as the education in public Black, Colored and Asian schools was inferior and barely up to standard. The deciding factor came when my oldest daughter, Vidisha, was graduating with honors in her seventh-grade class and received first-place awards in all six subjects. The school awarded a cup for each subject. She had to go up with a white girl who had scored ten points less than she did to receive her prize. It was improper for an Asian to receive the cups alone.

The following week, my husband and three of his staff were beaten and tied up in our retail shop by four men armed with knives and daggers. They left taking $25,000 in cash and goods. This really shocked us all. Our twins had been in the shop looking for scotch tape a few minutes before this happened. It made me realize how close I came to endangering my children's lives. The very next month, we began to plan to leave South Africa. This was a very heart-breaking decision, especially for me, as I was the youngest of eight in a very close-knit family. I had never been away, nor was I used to being alone or independent.

It was very sad leaving all the family and friends behind, not knowing what we were getting into, but we were hopeful. My husband's brother in Houston, Texas, was going to help us settle in. My father-in-law had gone ahead to find a motel business for us in the town of Brownwood. Imagine my shock when I saw Brownwood! It was situated in the heart of Texas with a population of 15,000 and it seemed to be the middle of nowhere! The people were so backward and prejudiced that I wondered if I had really left apartheid at all. They had no idea where South Africa was located: they thought we wore skins and ran around in jungles with the animals. There were only two other Indian families in Brownwood. Can you imagine moving from busy Johannesburg to this quiet town, where every day felt like Sunday and time felt like eternity? I wept most of the time and felt very lonely.

My husband hated the place. He missed his friends and the evening clubs that he frequented in Johannesburg, and he began getting temperamental with us. I occupied myself with the children's activities and tried to mix with their friends' parents. I used to wear only saris and had a nose ring, but when people stopped to stare at me like I was from another planet, I changed to Western clothes.

At first, the children were considered nerdy and the others teased them about it. Sarita and Anil would come home in tears after being called Dark Chocolate and Milk Duds. Sometimes they cried because they missed the home and family we had left behind. It was a period of adjustment for them, but it was not too long before they started settling. They enjoyed the new freedom of being able to go out on their own, making new friends, and they were adjusting to the school system. Anil became quite popular in class and his being a vegetarian evoked a lot of curiosity.

My three older children, Vidisha, Sangeeta and Aparna, also took some time to adjust. They raised their hands in school and spoke only when spoken to. They wore good clothes with matching shoes and socks, which the others thought was funny. However, my children were horrified at the rudeness and dressing of the other school kids, who ran in hallways, screamed at one another and were very casual to their teachers. There seemed to be no discipline of any sort around the school. Vidisha, my oldest, had a gang of boys who followed her around, teasing her and calling her names like Voodoo, suggesting we did black magic.

It wasn't long before the three started to feel more settled in. They all changed their style of dressing and tried to participate in a lot of the school activities. In fact, Sarita and Anil's principal called me to her office one day. Apparently, her daughter was expecting her first child, and she was impressed by my children and wanted to know what I had eaten during my pregnancy! I explained our Indian diet to her.

I made friends with Sunita and Gaiwant, one of the other Indian families. We shopped together and ate at each others' homes quite a bit. Sunita was quite a talented cook when it came to Italian or Mexican food. Meanwhile, my husband refused to be a part of any of this, and things deteriorated between us. We didn't have much communication to begin with, but I had thought leaving our friends and family in South Africa might bring us closer together. Instead, we had terrible rows and yelled at each other when the kids were out. He swore at me all the time, blaming me and the children for making him leave home, forgetting that it was he who was held up.

The worst day came when Anil had severe stomach cramps with high fever. I took him to the doctor. The pediatrician wanted me to take him to the hospital immediately — she thought it was appendicitis. I was scared because we had no insurance and I knew nothing of the system here. My husband refused to come to the hospital with us, saying it was my job to take care of the kids. I took the doctor's desk clerk with me. The hospital wanted tons of paperwork filled out relating to our income and so on, of which I knew nothing.

Eventually my son was admitted. The doctor wanted to operate on him. I was scared and called my father-in-law in California. He suggested that I should insist on a second opinion. The doctor was angry, but brought in another surgeon. This one took more blood tests before eventually giving Anil some strong antibiotic and anti-inflammatory medication and telling us to watch him overnight. The next day it was as if nothing had happened. Anil's temperature of a hundred and three degrees was normal and he was running around with his sisters. I was horrified to think I could have had surgery done on him. After this incident, I did everything on my own or asked my father-in-law, but my husband and I barely said any words to each other.

By this time, our business was going downhill. My husband blamed the declining number of clients coming to the motel on discrimination, but I also knew that his rudeness and bad attitude did not help either. He was grouchy and complained about the town to every customer. Then came the oil crisis, which hit Texas in a big way. Thousands of people lost their businesses and had to leave. The quiet little town now became a ghost town. Soon our mortgage payments became a problem and my father-in-law realized that we had to give up the business. I told him about how bad I felt and he said that as long as everyone was well, it was fine. Money was something we could always make again.

Our visa call could not have come at a better time. We were all miserable and depressed because of the business, so the thought of going home for six weeks seemed wonderful to us. The tickets were sent from home and we were on our way. Yet most of us didn't have a great time there. The children and I felt quite restricted. We had to be driven everywhere and could not do anything on our own. It was unsafe to go out alone during the day and at night everything was closed. I was thrilled to be with my family again, but soon I started feeling choked. My brother would check me each time I went to town to make sure I wasn't wearing any valuable jewelry. He was terrified for my safety. Only my husband really enjoyed himself. He spent most of his time with his friends.

After six weeks we were ready to leave, and this time it was for good. We packed seven big boxes with books, china and all our precious mementos, seven big bags of clothes and seven big pieces of hand luggage, but still had tons of stuff remaining. My brother-in-law and his wife had to get rid of it later on. My husband was not too happy to leave. He refused to help with any of the loading, so the children and I pushed, shoved and pulled the luggage all the way from New York International to La Guardia to Dallas. My father-in-law met us at the airport. Then he and my husband left to find a business in a bigger and better city where the children could go to college.

The children and I were on our own. I drove them to and from school, attended all their extra activities, cooked and ate what we wanted. We went for walks every evening with our friends and went to the mall on weekends. I caught up with my reading. It was the best year we had.

Then my father-in-law found a Howard Johnson motel for us in Tampa, Florida. We bought a four-bedroom house in Carrollwood Village. My sister-in-law, Gayatri, and her husband, Pankaj, helped us move. There were tons of Indian families, so we had no problem with Indian programs and functions. The children started their new schools.

My life revolved around the children. I cooked, cleaned and catered for the family and then helped at the motel. I would do the laundry and check on the maids and then be home when the children came from school. My husband and I separated. He lived on his own in an apartment, and came home once a week to pick up his food. I continued cooking

135

for him, as I did not want to upset my in-laws.

Over the years we had business problems again. The Howard Johnson franchise wanted everything new so we spent a lot on repairs. Then another motel opened within a mile of us. We decided to sell and once more were without a business. This time round, we lost a quarter of a million dollars. Pankaj and my father-in-law went to South Africa and sold all the property and businesses we had there. They could not bring the money back here. Meanwhile, the South African currency, the rand, was dropping fast because of political instability. It was losses all around.

One by one, my five children finished high school, then left home to pursue their education. I was now without any real work. This is when I ventured out into the work force for the first time. My mother-in-law was not happy at all because I was the oldest daughter-in-law, and she wanted me to sit at home with her. My first job was with a retail business, where I started off being a receiver, then was promoted to lay-away and finally to customer assistance. At work I met Janice, a wonderful person who was the supervisor for Children and Families Protective Services. In time, she offered me a job as a receptionist at her office. I was happy to accept because I knew there was no future for me in retail. I asked her if I could start after two months, as I was taking the four girls to India for the first time.

She agreed. Off we went on our trip, a trip that I paid for from my salary. I had never before felt such a sense of achievement or independence. I did all our bookings, made the necessary arrangements for our trip. The girls loved South India, with all its art, carvings and sculptures. They hated the dirt and overpopulation.

I started my new job the day after we returned. Janice included me in all her unit meetings where each case was discussed. I was horrified at the neglect and abuse that went on. Soon enough I knew every case history. I answered thirty phone lines and arranged all the meetings. I was seeing a different side of existence. Was it possible that a mother could leave her child outside in winter without food and warm clothing? Or a father could molest his own daughter or give his son drugs? I soon realized that most of these families went through the whole system of food stamps, Medicare, juvenile problems and protective services. I felt sorry for the counselors because they had to take children from families and put them in foster care. It was a difficult decision, and we all took part in discussing the pros and cons. I felt privileged to be a part of this staff.

Then my mother-in-law fell ill. She developed hypertension and was diagnosed with a kidney problem. I had to transfer into town so I could be closer to home. It was quite hard for me to leave Janice and the others. We had grown so close in the two years that I had worked there. This time I got a job with the Department of Juvenile Justice dealing with the offenders of Hillsborough County. My job, with five others, was to type all the data from the Sheriff's office and put it into the computer for the counselors. It was amazing how the same names popped up over and over. I saw some of the worst crimes committed by juveniles. It made me appreciate our Indian culture and upbringing.

Still unwell, my mother-in-law decided that she wanted to visit her family. The doctor advised my father-in-law to take her. They stayed in India for six months. As soon as they returned, they left again. My father-in-law wanted to build another motel because the one he built for his youngest son was so successful. He bought a piece of land in Houston and started from scratch. He was investing the last bit of money he had from South Africa and Tampa. In July, my mother-in-law became very ill. They came back. Her four sons and their families all came home to be with her. My son and I performed all the prayers for her last rites. The girls had taken a week off from college. At the end of August, she passed away. She had a very peaceful, painless death. My father-in-law and my brother-in-law, Pankaj, went back to Houston and started building the motel.

All this time, my husband still lived on his own and never supported us in any way. He felt sorry for himself and blamed everyone else for his problems. I was cooking once every two weeks for him now. He came home, took his food and walked out. I finally plucked up the courage to divorce him.

Someone once asked me if I ever regretted coming to the US. My unhesitant answer was "no." My children would not have learned about the world or themselves like they did here. They did become overly independent, but that is the price one pays for knowledge. In South Africa, we were too sheltered from everything. Here, one has to fend for oneself.

When I look back at my life in South Africa, I realize that my thinking has changed drastically. I don't feel that a girl has to be married by eighteen or twenty, nor do I feel that females were put on earth to serve the needs of their husbands or the male species. Now, I can live with the fact that my daughter may not marry or marry out of caste.

My father-in-law asked me to come to Houston. I agreed only after I was promised a share in the family business. I thought I would like to leave the children some legacy of my own.

✿ ✿ ✿

Être/Avoir

Nina Asher

I am
mild-mannered, brown, Asian.

You are
in your country of origin, owning the language.

She/It/He
is in the academy — our meeting place —
where we locate ourselves, only on different planes.

We are,
I find, crossing swords, not paths,
words, not minds.

You all are
congratulating even as you are thinking —
she took that job, could've been mine!

They are
very thorough at that girls' academy in Bombay
where I first learned the rules of English and French grammar.

I have
mild-manneredly, of course, put that English grammar to
good use.

You have
the status quo — your right of way, you believe.

She/It/He has
a lot to offer — but then there is so much to learn/teach
in the academy, no?

We have
our intellectual quests, our openness to new knowledge
as our common ground.

You all have
to agree — so kind — even as you feel for your birth-right.
mine, of course, isn't in question.

They have
to check their grammar — or is it language? Or, perhaps,
it is a question of vision — when the subject is an-other.

I am
mild-mannered, browner-than-ever,
(it's the June sun, what else) and the author.

🦋 🦋 🦋

From Africa to Canada: A Lesbian Family in Search of Home

Jo Goodwill

RECENTLY, our family went camping near Kelowna, British Columbia. My partner, Liza, and I watched as our two daughters, Emily and Kacie, played in the park near our camping cabin. The girls were wearing matching bright yellow overalls and blue T-shirts. They are going through a stage of pretending to be twins.

Of course no one thinks they're twins because Kacie is a big, stocky seven-year-old, while Emily is a tall and wiry four. Emily wears her hair in short braids, budding dreadlocks, and likes to adorn it with butterflies and bows. Kacie prefers her black curls shaved short, no-nonsense tomboy style. Sometimes we ask her if she would like to try braids or dreads, and she raises her arms defensively and says emphatically, "Nothing with the hair!"

We bought the yellow overalls in South Africa and the girls wore them on the plane when we came here. Now, a year and a half later, the girls are taller and the overalls too short. Liza has cleverly cut the overalls off at the knees, turning them into shorts. They are still brilliantly yellow, with the vibrant color of fabrics made under Africa's relentless sun.

The girls swung upside-down on the swings, their heads almost touching the ground, their whoops piercing the peaceful mountain air. I said to Liza, "You know, they're the only children of color in this whole resort, yet they're totally unselfconscious, just having a great time. I think it's because no one finds them strange, no one stares at them."

Liza looked thoughtful, then she said, "Well, the point is, no one questions their right to be here."

We both fell silent for a while, thinking how horrible this camping experience would have been in our home country. Post-apartheid South Africa retains the heritage of its ugly past, and is still no place for a multiracial family. Many people — usually white people — object strenuously at the sight of a racially mixed group or family. Transracial adoption has only been legal in South Africa since the end of 1991, and it is still rare enough to evoke confusion or hostility.

Kacie was born just two months after the abolition of the Population Registration Act. In terms of this act, babies had to have their race recorded on their birth certificates and in the population register. Their designation would then dictate where they could live, eat, work, go to school — even whom they could sleep with and marry. If Kacie had been born two months premature, it would not have been possible to adopt her. We wouldn't even have been able to take her home and await a change in the legislation because, at that time, apartheid was still in force. People of different races couldn't live in the same areas, let alone the same house.

Between 1991 and 1995, the laws, the constitution and the government changed dramatically. Nelson Mandela was released from prison and many of us looked forward to a better future. But the hearts and minds of people trained and indoctrinated to be racists have not changed as quickly. Many people, particularly white people who have lost much of their privilege, resent the changes bitterly. For them, I suppose, our family was a painful reminder of how much South Africa has changed. We never felt safe outside our front door — or inside, for that matter.

And that's why we came all the way to Canada. We flew exactly halfway around the world — if we'd gone any further we'd have been on our way home again. Our family structure would be unusual anywhere: there's me, a thirty-nine-year-old lesbian, and then there's my lover, Liza, who's twenty-seven. We're the moms. Then there are our two adopted daughters, Kacie and Emily. Liza and I are white; our daughters are black. So we're a multiracial lesbian family. We were living in South Africa, still one of the most conservative, homophobic and racist countries in the world. We were finding it impossible to be a family. We came to Vancouver, driven by a need to find a community we could call home. A place where we would not be the freaks on the block; where people wouldn't stare at us in perplexity or anger.

And yet there was more than that; deep in our hearts, we nursed the seemingly impossible dream of finding a place where we would not merely be tolerated. We hoped to find a home where we would be welcomed, accepted and respected. We did a lot of research and decided to try Vancouver, British Columbia, Canada — a place we had never seen before. Now is a good time to look back and decide whether we did the right thing.

To get here, we had to endure a nine-hour flight, a ten-hour stopover in London, and then an eleven-hour flight. While the children slept soundly most of the way, the moms had time to reflect on the enormity of what we were doing, and on just how far it actually was. On the little globe back home, it hadn't seemed nearly so terrifying. We had left behind us the glorious sunshine of Africa in summer. We arrived in Vancouver on an icy, drizzly night in mid-January. Dirty sludge lay on the ground from a light snowfall the day before. We were exhausted, the temperature was precisely zero, and we didn't know a single person on the whole continent. We had to go through immigration at the airport. Fortunately, that turned out to be a very pleasant experience. We waited for just a few minutes and were processed quickly and efficiently by a friendly official. "Welcome to Canada. What beautiful children you have," he said with a big smile. I wonder if he has any idea how much his greeting helped.

Like many immigrants, we then collected our entire worldly possessions, tightly crammed into eight suitcases. Getting to a taxi was difficult for two women weighed down

143

by 500 pounds of luggage and two small, sleepy children. We had to take a limousine, as this was the only vehicle big enough to accommodate all of us. And so we arrived in style, if somewhat exhausted and bedraggled, at our new home. We had managed to organize a sublet of a furnished apartment in an East Vancouver co-op. We lived there for six months before securing our own spot in another co-op nearby.

After we arrived, it rained solidly for nineteen days. We became worried that there was no sun in the northern hemisphere! It was hard not to be a little depressed, especially as we were also being overwhelmed by a tidal wave of strangeness. We kept forgetting that cars traveled on the right-hand side of the road, so that even crossing the roads was hazardous for us. We would go to shops or banks and find them still closed, because Canada wakes up later than South Africa. Going outside the house was a complicated maneuver, involving the unfamiliar process of dressing the children and us in layers of clothing, gloves, hats and coats. Shopping was a protracted nightmare, with stores stocked with an overwhelming variety of unknown brands, so that the simplest trip could take ages. Without a car, we had to dive headfirst into a first-world public transport system, and this was quite challenging. Liza found it less frightening than I did. To me, the skytrain felt like something out of a sci-fi novel. On the other hand, we kept marveling at being able to use the system without fear of attack. We were also amazed at its efficiency and reliability.

Wherever we went, everything and everybody was strange. A simple activity like taking the kids to McDonald's was confusing and humiliating, as we couldn't understand the questions being fired at us in Canadian accents. We had to go through a process of decoding both the accents and the terminology, discovering that what we called chips were fries here and that tomato sauce was now ketchup. "Would you like to come with us to the drug store?" our neighbor asked us on our second day.

"No thanks, I don't think we need any drugs," I replied.

Liza hurried over to tell me that she thought a "drug store" was actually a general grocery store and that we really did need to go.

Everything felt slow and exhausting, like swimming against the tide. I was thirty-seven; in South Africa I had been a mature woman, confident and successful. Here, in this strange, huge city, I suddenly felt overwhelmed, disempowered and ignorant again, like a small child lost in a strange neighborhood where the people speak a different language. The feeling of powerlessness would sometimes threaten to overwhelm me completely. I would feel furious at my own incompetence and long to go back, where I could again be in control.

Driving in a car would bring home the foreignness of it all. Shops and streets and buildings would flash by endlessly, every one of them strange to us. Nothing was familiar; nothing reflected us or held memories of our past. I felt like Venus, rising full-grown from the ocean with no past and an unknown future. Walking wasn't much better. This gave me time to see people in the distance coming towards me, sometimes a person who looked like someone I knew. My spirits would leap in anticipation of meeting an old friend. Then, as the person drew closer and the lines of their face grew clearer, they would inevitably turn out to be just another stranger. I longed for someone to break into a warm smile and say, "Hello."

My daughter Kacie started kindergarten. Being big, plump, tomboyish and African, she managed to stand out, even on the multicultural playing fields of the elementary school we chose. Sometimes we would walk past the school at lunchtime and see her in the distance, a small, lonely figure, head downcast, hands in pockets, kicking disconsolately at stones. A still figure in the whirling midst of other kids having fun together. It was wrenching, and more than anything else, it made me want to take us all home.

Still and all I am happy that we came, and quite certain

that we're not going back to South Africa. Starting with that official at immigration, all of our experiences as an alternative family have been positive. During the first week, we went down to the local community center. We wanted to join as a family. Back in South Africa, no one had ever accepted that we were one, so I sailed into the community center in full attack mode, ready to defend our right to be treated as a family. The wind was completely taken out of my sails when the clerk responded to our request for the membership with a simple, "That'll be five dollars," and a friendly smile.

This experience has been repeated many times. For a long time I was pathetically grateful each time we were accepted as what we are — a family. Now, after a year, I've grown accustomed to being welcomed and respected for what we are. I simply couldn't go back to the way it was in South Africa, where our self-identification as a family evoked either incomprehension (at best) or hostility (at worst). It was bad enough that we were a lesbian family, and thus so rare as to be invisible. What made our lives far more difficult was being so obviously a mixed-race family.

In South Africa, mixed-race couples and families are rare, and they learn to be careful about where they show themselves in public. Verbal and physical attacks are common. I was once walking down the street, pushing Kacie — then nine months old, and surely the most beautiful baby girl in the world — in her stroller. Two street people walked past me, reeking of stale urine and cheap wine. They peered into the stroller in disgust, and then the man drew himself up to his full height and barked at me disapprovingly, "Madam moet daardie vuilgoed weggooi!" (Madam should throw away that trash.) The man was of mixed race, lighter than my child was, but darker than I was. Thus, he addressed me as madam, in deference to the fact that I was whiter than he was. But he perceived my precious baby as garbage, as she was "more black" than he. In South Africa, racism is complex, multi-layered and ubiquitous. Life is not pleasant for those who dare to flaunt the rules.

Just before we emigrated, we took a final holiday in South Africa. Because of family considerations, we visited a conservative coastal town. I was not optimistic about it, but did hope to take a last swim in the warm Indian Ocean, in which I had spent many of the happiest hours of my youth. My misgivings proved justified: I hated the holiday, as we were stared at everywhere we went. Not for being lesbians, as this was not obvious — simply for being a mixed race group. The girls in particular stood out because they were well dressed, clearly well fed and spoke English so well (despite political changes, most black South Africans still live far below the poverty line). I tried to hide my discomfort and fear so that the children could enjoy the holiday. But one morning, Kacie and I went down to swim in a tidal pool beside the sea. Kacie's had swimming lessons since she was nine months old and swims with power and delight. It was early morning and only a few senior white citizens were out, sitting on the benches and staring at us with uncomprehending hostility. I could almost hear them thinking: "We've been swimming in this pool for fifty years and we've never seen a black person in it. What the hell is going on here?"

Kacie, who was then six and usually blissfully oblivious of other people's reactions to her, suddenly said to me, "I don't like it here. I feel as if everyone is staring at me and it makes me nervous."

That sentence summed up our family's experience in South Africa. Well, none of us has ever had occasion to express that concern since we've lived near Commercial Drive. Indeed, such is the diversity of life here that it is difficult to imagine what one would have to do if one *wanted* to be stared at!

Obviously, everything is not perfect here. We have had some problems, and some experiences of ignorance. We know that homophobia and racism live here too. After all, we arrived here in the middle of an attempt by the Surrey School Board to keep three utterly innocuous books out of their schools, purely because they portrayed same-sex families. Still, despite such anomalies, it is by and large a paradise for us. I have got to know the good in Canadians. I find their politeness endearing and their friendliness infectious. I have learned to find their accents comprehensible, even charming. And I love them for so generously offering me and mine a place in their smoothly operating society. I have never before experienced a society that works this well, and I am in constant awe. And so many people have warmly opened their hearts and homes to us. We have made many good friends with relative ease and no longer feel lonely and isolated. Wherever we go, people break into a warm smile and say, "Hello." Sometimes it feels as if we've lived here all our lives.

Liza has found a job she enjoys, while I am concentrating on taking care of the children and helping them to adjust to their new country. They are now well settled in. Kacie doggedly went off to school every day, bravely fighting her lonely battle for acceptance in her strange new world. She is by nature gentle, outgoing and gregarious, and has now succeeded in making many new friends. She is popular both at school and in our co-op, and is doing well with her schoolwork and enjoying the diversity of activities and sports that Vancouver offers. Little Emily is happily participating in swimming, gymnastics and various drop-ins. She appears to love her life here. In the beginning, she spoke daily of her beloved uncles and aunts and grandparents, but that has begun to fade now. That makes us sad and we hope to visit South Africa before her memories of family fade completely.

Apart from wanting to find a place that felt like home, we also came here to give our children a chance to grow up in a society that works. Back in South Africa, they were learning to lock their doors against the world; to trust nobody, because anybody could rob and kill you any moment. They were learning to stay close to their moms because we were living in the rape capital of the world, with one woman being attacked every eight seconds. South Africa bears horrible scars from its oppressive past and the society is terribly distorted. Nothing works properly and it will take the new government many years to repair the harm done by the previous regime. Here in Canada, we live in a supportive co-op with many other families.

Our girls are learning to open the door because the knock on the door probably means a neighbor has come to visit or play, or perhaps to give you something they no longer need. They are learning that human beings can live together harmoniously and that most people can be trusted. They are mixing with people who see them simply as regular children. It is extraordinarily difficult for most people in South Africa to see beyond color.

The other morning, Kacie chose to wear an African outfit that we had brought with us from South Africa. It is now a good few inches too short for her. Walking behind her on the way to school, I looked at her ankles poking awkwardly out of the multicolored pants. My girl has grown Canadian ankles, I thought. And as time goes on, all of her will become Canadian. Already, she sounds a lot like the other kids on the playground. She and Emily will not remember Africa and it is a fathomless loss. But they will be Canadians, living safely in a community that welcomes and nurtures them, and I believe that will make it all worthwhile.

South Africa is still home, a beautiful one, with the vibrant intensity and depth that is quintessentially Africa. But we can never forget that it is also a hostile home, where we were not wanted. So we work on making Vancouver our home. It isn't that difficult. I have never loved a neighborhood as much as I love East Vancouver, with its kaleidoscopic assortment of people and lifestyles. The warm, strong smell of Italian coffee nestles snugly against the rich spicy odor of Jamaican chicken, right across the road from the mingling aromas of Vietnamese and Mexican cuisine. Somehow, all manage to live together in a harmonious, heterogeneous neighborliness. This is not like the stark separations of our own apartheid-driven country, where we created a family that stuck out like an elephant in a crow's

149

nest — and had about the same chance of survival.

I grew up as an isolated misfit because I never could understand the need to hate everyone who was different. This incomprehension was no doubt fuelled by my secret knowledge of myself as Other, because I knew from the age of five that I was never going to fit neatly into the heterosexual world I saw around me. Through all those years, I consoled myself with the fantasy that I must have been dropped off by people from another planet. That was why I was such a hopeless misfit. But it would be all right, because one day my real people would come to take me home. Since I have been in Canada, that fantasy has faded a lot. I am starting to believe that I have found my real people; that here in Vancouver, Canada, this thirty-nine-year-old lesbian mom has finally come home.

※ ※ ※

Desire

Christl Verduyn

I wanted my life
to be like
other people's.

I wanted it to be
what I saw through
windows at nightfall.

I wanted it
Transparent.
Apparent.

A pair of parents
and I the apple
of their eye.

Not myself
looking in
from outside.

❦ ❦ ❦

Untitled Poems

Rosita Ferrero de Estable
(translated by Alma Estable)

I

It is not always necessary
to have the sense of time
to arrive at the exact hour
without gathering up memories.

Sometimes ... it is necessary
to wander on the wings of time
gathering up pebbles,
leaves and pieces of soul.

Making a bouquet with them
and losing oneself on the paths.
Can one's way be found on these?

Sometimes ... it is necessary
to let the wind's wound
sink the dagger in your flesh,
temper you in blood and steel.

You will understand the silence.
You will understand the words.
You will leap to the other bank
of the river of confusion
of the rivers that escape
from the veins of your body.

II.

I have a pain in my breast.
A cry that becomes a river.
A dream that becomes wind.

My blood which nourishes the river
my soul which cradles the dream.

I have a pain in my breast
and I want to set it free
transforming it
into a bouquet of red carnations
so that it becomes an eternal carpet
to the soul that cradles the dream
to the dream that becomes wind.

III

In this small space
there is also life
and there are dreams
disillusions and hopes
voices of eternal songs
hands that interlace
questions that I only feel
when in your eyes I enter
and arrive to the depths of a soul
that suffers without complaint.

Do you know what?
At times, I also feel it.
I invite you:
open wide the window,
we will cast out that which ties.
Without brakes,

we will leap
purified in the frozen wind
of a no-tomorrow.
Let us leave in eternal flight.

Does it frighten you?
I am afraid.
Let us think again ...

Let us build other bridges
with a present and a tomorrow.
We cannot remain still.

I feel,
and we are,
like two dolls
whom someone wound up
and abandoned.
And we walk,
and we stop,
and we wait.

Do you know what?
Let's not wait for someone to arrive.
We are two in this space.
Helping each other, let us walk.
You know, we have arms.
You know, we have hands.

And we are two hearts,
two minds,
and one past.

If one winds up the other
we can keep on going,
and we will face the wind
taking those first steps.

If there is snow,
what do we care?
Walking we will go, playing,
our steps do not have wings.
Look ... do you see?
The tracks we are leaving behind?

It is the weight of the years.
I think and believe
that they are the footsteps of destiny,
so that we will not forget
when we turn our heads to look back,
the path already walked.

A deep feeling
of this body and this soul
that at times seem like strangers
is to think, to know
that they are yours and they are mine
in the present and in the past.

Do you know? I say it again,
I tell myself, and how I know it!
And it pleases me to think
how, when we turn our heads to look back,
we will see
always together
our footsteps.

IV

I feel that I don't feel and I feel

I have just lived
Lorca again,
in this year
more his than ever.

And his women dance
and my wonder increases.

I rediscover them in memories
as strong characters
with the strength of the Spain
told by my grandparents

with the dreams of the Spain
that are still in my breast.
And I wonder at my wonder
Is it that I
          do not understand them?

From where comes that strength
so that honeyed eyes
transform into steel
so that bodies of straw
arise with stars
only flesh, bone
          and blackness
only flesh, red
          and fire.

And I feel that Lorca is colors
but red, white
          and black
And I feel that Lorca is screams
          that escape from the breast.

And I feel that I feel
and I don't feel
And I feel that I don't feel
and I feel ...

And I feel that Lorca
is hands clapping

in the precise moment
and I feel that Lorca
is silence
     that follows the silence ...

And I feel that Lorca
is the soul
that clings tightly to the body
that sways
in dances
with movements of steel
that sways
in dances
with flashes of fire
where souls melt
separating from the body
each dance, each their own dance
body, magic and
       mystery

Wizardry of the earth
Witchery of the skies

Ay!! the strength of the Spain
that has populated my dreams.

Ay!! the strength of the Spain
that you have shown me recently.

Thanks, thanks gives my soul.

Thanks, thanks gives my body.

And where did Lorca remain?
And his women of steel?
Of black and of white,
of red and of fire ...

They are no longer only brown-skinned,
as they were in my memories.
Next to the young ones are others
with the burden of the years
bent with memories.

The women who work
and who dance ...
      only in dreams.

Women who raise their children.
their bodies are not of straw
and in their eyes
yes, there is light
but missing
are the flashes of steel.

And in their eyes, there is light
of sun, moons, and stars

Their reds are the geraniums
the carnations
      and even the bush of their hair
the sun and the fire in the afternoon
the brilliance of the skies.

these women are others
these women of the Spain
sung by my grandparents.

And I feel that I feel
and I don't feel
And I feel that I don't feel
and I feel ...

V

White and empty remained the page
white and in silence
in suspended flight
in hollows of mystery
in rhythms not sung
in times of other times.

White and empty remained the page
while you were grinding
in the mortar of hopes,
the screams and silences,
sorrows and mysteries,
the blood of rough struggle,
the balance of a kiss,
the memory of memories
that were peeking
through the windows of sleep
between mountains of foam
and scribbles of ice.

White and empty is not the page.
It is already full of dreams.

VI

The girl is a child.
Let her play
let her laugh and dance,
let her, let her
with her long skirt
put on haphazardly,
and large hoop earrings.
At times it seems

that she lives
balancing
future and
past.

Dreaming the steps,
she already hears applause.

The girl is a child.
Leave her, leave her,
to invent memories
to dream of the present
to fly to the future.

When, smiling,
she curtsies,
let her, let her.

VII

As the day nears its end
we glide
on roads of cement
bordered by fields
farms, little houses of dreams,
scattered woods
and at a distance, the mountains.
Contours that transform themselves
borders that become clear outlines
contrasting with the sky.

The mountains regain
the relief of their breasts.
Roads are pencilled in,
and silhouettes in the sky.

Their peaks are no longer white.
There is red, violet and black
there are castles of dreams
and stairways in the sky
there are dragons and ghosts
elephants and giraffes
and giants with tender eyes.

And we keep on devouring
roads and villages
and we see the lights go on
on the earth and in the sky
and the road darkens
and suddenly
the great silence.

❧ ❧ ❧

Origins

Mariam Pirbhai

Heading home

we fly
everywhere nowhere
an imaginary flight
back to
where [do] you come from
an overdose of origins
through blood and tides

home
clings to the contours of continents
shifts with the shadows of sand dunes
adrift on the outskirts of tropical torrents

home
trips over mountains
skips over rivers like stone

home
dies with the sigh of a memory lost
eclipsed by a crescent on sundays
a prayer we recite
with rose-scented ritual
and press
like a leaf between
poems of

home.

❧ ❧ ❧

Contributors

Asha Asher is an occupational therapist, with a master's degree from the University of Southern California. She migrated to Canada in 1989 with her husband, bringing her children over in 1990, after which the family took up Canadian citizenship. A job transfer moved the family to the United States.

Nina Asher is an assistant professor in the Department of Curriculum & Instruction in the College of Education at Louisiana State University, Baton Rouge. In addition to research and teaching, she is involved with the Department's Curriculum Theory Project and is a faculty member in Women's and Gender Studies at LSU. She has written about the negotiation of identities and representations particularly in relation to Asian American education and women of color in the academy. Her publications include articles on syncretic music as a vehicle for re-negotiating South Asian diasporic identities, and the significance of self-reflexivity in research and writing as a woman academic of color.

Antara Chakraborty is Indian, born in Kenya in 1982. Her parents, Bijan Kumar and Papiya are from Calcutta, India. Antara spent thirteen years of her life in Aleppo, Syria. She migrated to Canada in June 1998. She's met commendable people, but still her friends in Canada are unknown to her.

Shamila N. Chaudhary is completing an Arts and Sciences Bachelor's degree in English and Women's Studies at the University of Toledo. She co-ordinates volunteer activities at the Sexual Assault Education and Prevention Program at the university. Shamila's research interests include the construction of gender in Indian cinema; educational histories of urban and rural Pakistani women; gender equity

165

in education in the United States; and incorporating Women's Studies in high schools. Shamila plans to pursue graduate study in South Asian Studies, Women's Studies and Public Policy.

Fatima Correia is currently studying at the Ontario Institute for Studies in Education and is immersed in writing her doctoral thesis on adolescent girls and weight preoccupation. This thesis preoccupies her time, mind and energy, and she hopes to emerge relatively unscathed from the process to begin work as a psychotherapist.

Dr. Rosita Ferrero de Estable was born in 1930 in Montevideo, Uruguay, as a second-generation child of Spanish immigrants. She married in 1952 and has four daughters, four sons and nine grandchildren. In 1966, her family immigrated to Canada, where Rosita continued her career as a medical researcher, an associate of the Medical Research Centre and a teacher in the Faculty of Medicine, Laval University, Quebec. With almost 200 publications in the field of pathology, experimental neuropathology and medical pedagogy, she retired in 1996.

Veena Gokhale is a writer, environmentalist, cinephile and party girl who has lived in Mumbai, Calcutta, Toronto (her favorite city) and other places. Among her great wishes: to have her short stories published and to have North Americans quit driving cars so there's free public transit everywhere. She is leaving Beautiful British Columbia to head back east, where she hopes to lead an idyllic existence with her lover.

Jo Goodwill has worked in publishing for most of her adult life. She and her family immigrated to Canada in January 1998. She is the author of several reference works, including *The Oxford Junior Dictionary for Southern Africa*. Her special interests include lesbian and women's issues and science fiction. Jo's partner, Liza, works at the Vancouver Public Library.

Sheela Haque is a US-born, first-generation American of Pakistani heritage in her second year of college on the East Coast, where she grew up. She argues, "I don't think that most people realize how Pakistani Muslims, especially first generation girls, are caught in a double struggle. We have to not only try to assimilate our traditional, sexist families with the more liberal, contemporary society that surrounds us, but we also have to try to obey a strict religion in a country where the values are very different and more open minded. If you are an 'Americanized pseudo-Muslim,' you don't feel a part of the Pakistani-Muslim culture, and if you are identified as a 'Pakistani Muslim in America,' you don't feel like a part of the American culture. Then there are those of us who waver between the two, never feeling completely at home anywhere. I believe that there can be a middle ground, that won't be reached without something important being compromised or diluted."

Chrystyna Hnatiw was born in Slovakia of Ukrainian parents. She arrived in Canada in 1949 and settled in Winnipeg. Chrystyna completed her M.A. in Slavic Literature at McMaster University and her education degree at the University of Manitoba. She has taught junior and high school in Manitoba. Some of Chrystyna's poetry and prose have appeared in English and Ukrainian publications.

Hope works with children. Her family migrated to Canada in 1989 and later relocated to the United States.

Jin Lee is a Korean-Canadian who was born in Seoul, South Korea and raised in Toronto, Ontario. Jin is pursuing an M.D./M.B.A. at Tufts University in Boston, where she resides.

Peggy Woon-Yee Lee is a Hong Kong Canadian now living, learning and doing resistance work in Hong Kong. Born in a British colony, she immigrated to yet another neo-colony (Canada) at the age of one. Twenty-odd years later, she chose to return to her birthplace at a moment when its colonizers were changing hands. Living in a city ravaged by imperialist capitalism, she is learning about courage through solidarity with the working people there.

Aida Mashari was fifteen years old when she wrote the poem in this anthology. Her family came to Canada in 1990, when she had just finished grade one, because of the political situation in Iran. As one can imagine, the distance is almost unbearable for her parents. This poem reflects the lifetime of gratefulness she feels toward her mother for this sacrifice.

Cristina Moretti was born and raised in Milan, Italy. She lived in Germany for two years and immigrated to Canada in 1992. As an anthropologist, she conducted research on women's life stories and the role of narrative in social movements. She currently works with different community groups in the areas of anti-racism and social justice. She writes poems in English and Italian.

Prabhjot Parmar has lived mostly in the Greater Vancouver area since immigrating from India nine years ago. Other immigrant women's experiences, combined with her own, have contributed to shaping her existing outlook. She has worked closely with women who have experienced violence in their lives. She received her Master's in English literature from Panjab University, India, and from Queen's University at Kingston. She attributes her strengths to her parents' progressive attitude toward equality and the fight for justice. Prabhjot passionately advocates for women's rights and human rights.

Mariam Pirbhai was born in Karachi, Pakistan in 1970. Since her family's emigration from Pakistan in 1975, she has lived in England, the United Arab Emirates, the Philippines and Canada. Mariam currently lives in Montreal where she is completing her Ph.D. in South Asian Diasporic Literature in English. She is also a lecturer at the University of Montreal and a Faculty Member at Vanier College. Invariably, Mariam's multiple homelands are the greatest impetus behind her creative writing and academic research. The poem in this anthology is part of a collection. The short story is part of her novel-in-progress, *The Naked Mind of Winter.*

Amal Rana is of Pakistani-Jewish descent.

Edith Samuel is a South Asian immigrant who has lived in Canada for the past nine years. She lives in Kingston and is currently working towards a doctorate degree in education at the Ontario Institute for Studies in Education in Toronto.

Nadia Sapiro is twenty-four years old and starting to pursue a career as a writer. She has not been back to visit South Africa since she left, but still maintains close ties with her friends and family still living there. Her aspiration is to live every day with passion.

Farah Mahrukh Coomi Shroff, Ph.D., is an activist, researcher, educator and mother. She lives in Vancouver, where her writing is inspired by forests, beaches, mountains and the laughter of baby Zubin.

Nila Somaia-Carten was born and raised in Kenya. Migration is not new to her family. Her father's side of the family is Hindu Gujarati, having moved to Kenya from India in the late 1800s. Her mother's family is Christian, from Mangalore, South India. Nila lived in the United Kingdom and the United States for a number of years before moving to Canada in 1992. She has an M.Ed. in counseling and lives in Vancouver. Her most recent interests include scuba diving and fencing.

Hoa Tran arrived in the United States in November 1975 from South Vietnam with her parents, four sisters and two brothers. Their travel took eleven months, staying at one refugee camp after another. The family settled in Atlanta, Georgia. Hoa is currently working on her Ph.D. in cultural anthropology. She has worked with Vietnamese refugees and immigrants for over ten years, and is very involved in community activism.

Christl Verduyn was born in the Netherlands and lives and works in Waterloo, Ontario. Her creative writing has appeared in *Grain*, *The Canadian Forum*, *Canadian Woman Studies*, *The New Quarterly*, *The Wascana Review*, *Backwater Review* and *Vintage*.

Lubna Warawra was born in the war-torn West Bank of Palestine during a military curfew. She grew up in Bethlehem and graduated in 1990 from the computer science department of Jordan University. After working as a software engineer for twelve years, she felt it was time to channel her artistic energy into composing poetry and prose. She has also explored the medium of film: her short film, *the departure the arrival*, was screened in the San Francisco Annual Arab Film Festival in 2001, and her film *I Would Die For You* is due to be screened at the 2003 Chicago Palestinian Film Festival. Lubna emigrated to Canada in 1996 and to the United States in September 2000.

Laurie Anne Whitt has had work published in various journals, including *The Spoon River Poetry Review*, *Puerto Del Sol*, *The Malahat Review*, *Wisconsin Review*, *Hawai'i Review*, *PRISM International*, *Cottonwood* and *Poetry Canada Review*. She lives on the Keweenaw Peninsula in Upper Michigan and teaches philosophy at Michigan Technological University. Her piece in this anthology, "My Lady-In-The-Cage," was first published in *Porcupine Literary Arts Magazine*.

Mehri Yalfani was born in Hamadan, Iran. She graduated from the University of Tehran in electrical engineering and worked as an engineer for twenty years. She started to write short stories when she was in high school. Her first collection of stories, *Happy Days*, was published in 1966. For almost fifteen years, raising three children and working full-time, she didn't have a chance to write. Then her novel *Before the Fall* was published in 1980. In 1987 she moved to Canada with her family, and since then she has published her works in many Farsi and English publications, such as *Fireweed* and *Dandelion*. Two collections of her short stories and three novels are in Farsi, her mother tongue. Her latest novel, *Afsaneh's Moon*, was published in 2002. She is currently translating her Farsi novels, *Far From Home* and *Dancing in a Broken Mirror*, into English.

※ ※ ※